‸TION

Kindergarten

Kindergarten

P. S. Rushforth

HAMISH HAMILTON . *LONDON*

9303

First published in Great Britain 1979
by Hamish Hamilton Ltd
Garden House, 57–59 Long Acre, London WC2E 9JZ

Copyright © 1979 by P. S. Rushforth

British Library Cataloguing in Publication Data

Rushforth, P. S.
  Kindergarten.
  I. Title
  823'.9'1F   PR6068.U7/
  ISBN 0–241–10263–4

Printed in Great Britain by
Willmer Brothers Limited, Rock Ferry, Merseyside

We only wanted to get away, only escape and arrive safely, nothing else.

Anne Frank. Wednesday, 8th July, 1942.

Whenever I close my eyes
I see them wander
There from this old farmhouse destroyed by the war
To another ruined house yonder.

High above them, in the clouded sky
I see others swarming, surging, many!
There they wander, braving icy blizzards,
(Homes and aims they haven't any)

Searching for a land where peace reigns,
No more fire, no more thunder,
Nothing like the world they're leaving,
Mighty crowds too great to number.

Bertolt Brecht. From *Children's Crusade*

For the people who gave me their words.

One

The faces in newspaper photographs and on television news-reports have changed. The faces of terrified children, and of women holding up imploring hands, are no longer South-East Asian faces, but the faces of Europeans. The gunfire, the burning buildings, the bomb explosions, are in the streets of European cities once again. The unknown possibilities of death are all around us.

It was Christmas Eve.

The terrorists in the West Berlin school were making the captive children sing carols.

Children's voices came across the waste of snow in front of the school, the distant mass of the buildings showing no light from its windows. At first, Corrie thought they were singing *The Red Flag* – the tune was the same – but then he made out the words.

> *O Tannenbaum, o Tannenbaum, wie treu sind deine Blätter!*
> *Du grünst nicht nur zur Sommerzeit,*
> *Nein, auch im Winter, wenn es schneit.*
> *O Tannenbaum, o Tannenbaum, wie treu sind deine Blätter!*
>
> *O Tannenbaum, o Tannenbaum, du kannst mir sehr gefallen:*
> *Wie oft hat nicht zur Weihnachtszeit*

1

Ein Baum von dir mich hocherfreut!
O Tannenbaum....

The group of terrorists at the school were from the same terrorist organisation, Red Phoenix, as the people who had carried out the shootings at Leonardo da Vinci airport. He felt his stomach beginning to tighten. He had switched on the television to watch a cartoon version of *Hansel and Gretel*, and the afternoon news-report immediately preceded the children's programme.

Lilli, who had come through into their kitchen from her house next door, walked into the living-room behind him, drawn in by the German words. He turned to face his grandmother.

'What is that song?'

'*Der Tannenbaum*. The fir-tree,' she answered quietly. The words had awoken memories for her.

He thought of the special television news-programme for the deaf on Sunday evenings, a digest of the week's events, when subtitles appeared at the bottom of the screen as the newscaster spoke.

Lilli sat beside him, looking at the television.

'The song tells us the fir-tree is a symbol of faith. It is always green, in summer, and in winter also, when it is snowing. We learn from it hope and steadfastness.' She pulled a face as she spoke the last word, and looked interrogatively at him.

He nodded. The word was right.

'The fir-tree is noble and alone. It comforts and strengthens us.'

She spoke each word very carefully, her mouth sometimes working awkwardly, as though the words were small solid objects she balanced between her lips. Her whole mouth puckered, as if she were about to pronounce the letter 'o', like a child's when it has sucked something sour. It was only in her speech that the stroke she had suffered eighteen months ago occasionally left its sign, though strangers would not have

2

noticed this, believing that her hesitancies were those of someone to whom English was a foreign language.

Her fingers were pulling the front of her smock.

'It was one of the few Christmas songs allowed in the time of Hitler. It makes no mention of Christ.'

He looked at her face. Physical pain always faded as time passed. The memory of humiliation and mockery never died. Each time it was thought about, the feelings returned as intense as they had been at the time they were first experienced.

She held her hand in front of him, opening out her fingers, and smiled.

'*Der Tannenbaum.*'

He picked up the slender green fir needles from her open palm, smelling their freshness – snow in dark forests – noticing, for the first time, other needles clinging to the front of her smock, and down her skirt.

'O Tannenbaum, o Tannenbaum,' he said, and began to pick other needles from Lilli's clothes, dropping them into his cupped left hand.

He had once been a little afraid of Lilli. She was tall, still considerably taller than he was, small for his age. She looked rather fierce, and now, in her seventies, was dressed in a loose billowing smock with a tiny dark floral pattern, and a rust-coloured floor-length velvet skirt. Her hair, still dark, hung loosely about her face, not like an old woman's at all. She looked like a folk-singer with a rich clear voice who would sing sad songs about the deaths of maidens, the cruelty of love, all the songs collected by his grandfather before his death. It was only in the last year that he had really talked to her, as he had helped to give her lessons after her stroke. His hands moved gently against the velvet material. Stroke. That was what a stroke was. A gentle touch of affection. A gentle touch on the brain that could cripple.

It was nine months since the killings in Rome. That had been during the Easter holidays. Mum would have been carrying Easter presents for them all. She had promised to get them all something.

3

The face on the television screen was a face at a window, the face of a frightened child. Below the child's face, the now familiar image behind the newscaster on each day's news, were the words *School Siege: Day Seven*. They were marking the end of the first week of the siege by an extended news-programme, the most coverage the event had had since the day it had started. As the number of days of the siege rose, news about the school had come later and later in news-reports, moved to the inside pages of newspapers, shorter and smaller as the days went by, compressed by the greater demands of more recent events: a bomb explosion in Tel Aviv, a shooting at a Middle Eastern embassy in Rome, a hijacked plane in Belgium. The same pictures appeared over and over again: the airliner on a lonely desert strip, viewed from a distance across bare sand; the hooded figure at the window with the submachine-gun. In the Sunday digest of the week's events on television, the words appeared and disappeared at the bottom of the screen, as if the words spoken were in a foreign language, talking of incomprehensible occurrences.

The second face on the television screen was that of a weeping woman, being restrained by a policeman wearing a peaked cap, as she tried to pull herself forward, and away from him, towards the encircled school, her eyes gazing upwards.

The newscaster began to talk about the political situation in West Germany.

Behind the newscaster as he continued speaking, filling the whole background, one brightly-coloured picture remained as an image of modern West Germany. A group of well-dressed people were sitting in a glass-enclosed street restaurant in a pedestrian precinct. Stainless-steel held the glass in place. It was very new, very sharp and shiny, like everything in the picture, the expensive clean impersonality of the transit-lounge of an international airport, where all the people there were only passing through. Behind the clean glass, wiped free of all fingerprints, the men and women ate elaborate ice-cream con-fections from narrow cone-shaped glasses, the laden spoons held before their open mouths. Their eyes had the shut,

4

closed-in look of people who knew they were being photo-graphed, but were trying to look natural. They all had rings on their fingers, men and women, and they were all middle-aged. Dim figures could be seen through the dark glass which closed off the inner rooms of the newly-painted building, many of them, but the door which led through from the outside, on which all the seated figures had their backs turned, was closed.

Inside his copy of *Grimm's Fairy Tales*, lying on the floor beside him on top of the notebook with the ruled staves, spidery with pencilled notes, crotchets and quavers, much corrected, was the postcard he had taken from The Ferry House. He had opened the door set into the bedroom wall, and gone into the room beyond.

The postcard had been posted in Berlin in June 1939, to the man who had then been the headmaster of Southwold School, a predecessor of his father.

Dear Mr High,

Thank you very much for your kind letter. I am so gratefull that you will receive me and my big brother in your school. We wait now for permits. I send you our good wishes. Dear Sir, also our parents thank you very much. Excuse, dear Mr High, all this troubles. Please pardon me about my stammerings, but my will is stronger than the words I know. We will be diligent in our study and becomingness, and prove ourselves worthy. We will be good boys. I am happy about my violoncello. Highly esteemed sir, I remain,

Yours respectfully,
Nickolaus Mittler.

Other pictures were shown on the television, some in colour, some in black and white: police-photographs of young men and women, unsmiling, staring straight ahead; photographs of bomb-damage; coffins being interred; bodies lying in streets, their feet protruding beyond the edges of the blankets; people

5

showing identity papers to policemen; film of riot-police with batons; crowds running from tear-gas; burning buildings. Film of that day's events at the West Berlin school was repeated, and the high children's voices came from out of the darkness and the unlit building.

Lilli held out her hand to take the fir-needles from him, and then stood up.

'How is the German Christmas?' he asked her.

She had spent the past week preparing what she said was going to be a 'traditional German Christmas' for them in her house, insisting on doing everything herself, keeping it all secret. Christmas Eve, she had told them, was the special, solemn time, when everything important happened. Christmas Day was not a special day. The fir-needles were a part of her plans. He had seen the fir-tree being delivered two days earlier. *Der Tannenbaum.*

'Six o'clock. The German Christmas will be ready at six o'clock.'

On the other side of the postcard was a sepia photograph. *Die Freilichtbühne, Berlin. (Open-air Theatre, Berlin.)*

The scene was an enormous open-air theatre built to the same design as the theatres of Ancient Greece. Tier upon tier of curved seating rose in an immense semi-circle away and upward from the circle of the orchestra, the dancing place for the Chorus. In the centre of that circle would be the altar. From the back centre point where the photograph was taken, the rows of seating arched away to right and left, the distant rows smaller and closer together. In the distance, behind the central grassed circle, was the acting area, a raised stone platform running the whole width from side to side, with a wide central flight of steps. Behind this was a high stone wall with a central entrance facing the centre of the flight of steps. Above and beyond the blank stone was a dark fir wood, its closely-packed trees tall and impenetrable, the inner darkness beginning only a few feet from the edge.

There was no human figure in the whole scene.

6

The thousands upon thousands of seats were empty, and the stage was deserted. It appeared as ruinous and abandoned as the ancient Greek theatres on which it was modelled, waiting for some call, some sacrifice, to fill all those seats with rapt and fascinated spectators, engrossed and involved in some great tragedy, to purge the emotions of pity and terror, Agamemnon sacrificing his daughter to help him win a battle, *The Trojan Women*, *The Bacchae*.

In such a drama, very few would speak, the leading actor would play several parts, surrounded by mute actors, and the identically-clad Chorus who moved in total unison. All deaths would take place off-stage, the slaughter of men, women, and children reported by a Messenger who would tell of what he had seen. Such drama was an act of worship, a reminder of the transience of man's life, a clear recognition of man's powerlessness in the face of mutability.

There would be the sound of a flute at sunrise, and through the central door on the raised platform, a figure larger than life-size, wearing a huge tragic mask, raised up on high-soled boots, would enter, and stand at the top of the flight of steps leading down into the circle. He would raise his head and look up at the tier upon tier of white faces surrounding him, rising higher and higher into the sky, before speaking the opening words of the tragedy which was to follow.

The boy who had written that postcard had the same surname as the two brothers in *Emil and the Detectives*, the boys Emil had met in Berlin. He remembered the younger brother, who usually never said a word, and the moment when everyone looked at him in amazement because he spoke – *Fish is so good* – and he flushed deep red and hid behind his big brother.

The figures in the restaurant reappeared. They all wore heavy coats, as if it were a cold country.

Lilli continued looking at the television screen, and then went towards the kitchen, her hand cupped around the gathered fir-needles.

7

'*Hansel and Gretel*?' he asked. He had told her that the cartoon was going to be on television, thinking it would interest her.

Lilli gave the suggestion her consideration, looking towards him.

She always looked with great intensity at whoever she was talking to, concentrating very seriously. He had seen her sitting and talking to Matthias, side by side, both unaware of their surroundings, looking very hard at each other, like two statesmen working together to solve an almost insurmountable world problem. Her eyes were a very bright blue, not faded, as you would expect in an old person: all the colours about her were rich and deep.

Slowly, she shook her head.

'No. I think not.' She smiled, a little sadly. 'No Hansel. No Gretel.' She spoke quietly. He turned to look at her face more closely, to recognise by her expression the quality of the emotion he had heard in her voice, but she had gone into the kitchen. Her voice came back to him, louder.

'The German Christmas will be ready at six o'clock.'

'The English cup of tea will be ready shortly.'

The news-report ended, and the faces behind the flawless glass faded.

The cartoon which followed was not the story of *Hansel and Gretel* he knew, the little boy and girl in the painting on his bedroom wall, the story he was trying to put into music.

The first third of the story, a section he remembered vividly from when he was young (Lilli's voice in his bedroom at The Dutch House, the sound of the sea in the background), Hansel and Gretel's realisation that their father and stepmother were taking them into the forest to be torn to pieces by wild animals, was completely omitted. The old woman in the gingerbread house was made a grotesque and hideous fiend, not an apparently normal old woman, helpful and kindly, the sort of person one could meet at any time; and it was not made clear

8

that Hansel and Gretel were going to be cooked and eaten by the old woman.

Like Humperdinck's opera, the story had been prettified and sentimentalised.

Some things were too frightening for children to know about, and who would wish to frighten children?

He switched off the television, and went into the kitchen. Lilli had gone through into her own house.

The style of the cartoon had borne little relation to the style of Lilli's illustrations for the story: the colours were garish, and the outlines crudely simplified. The precise detail and subtle colouring for which a Lilli Danielsohn water-colour was famous, were entirely missing.

The little boy, and the younger girl, stood hand in hand at the edge of an immense dark forest, towering high above them, dressed in the fashion of the 1930s, the little girl with an elaborately-woven shawl around her shoulders. They filled most of the picture, standing in the centre of the scene. The girl was looking in front of her, into the forest, and seemed frightened. The boy was looking over his shoulder, back the way he had come, looking straight into the face of anyone looking at the picture. The details were as intensely-observed as in a Victorian genre painting, and the boy's open, unguarded face could be studied in the detailed way that one could only give to a face in a painting or a photograph, or the face of someone who was loved, and who returned that love. He looked as though he were trying to memorise what was behind him. A few crumbs of bread were lying on the ground just behind him. On the outer side of the two children were the shadowy figures of adults, enclosing them, holding their arms, and leading them away.

Corrie was Lilli Danielsohn's grandson, the grandson of somebody famous, somebody who had been forgotten, and was being remembered again.

There had been a revival of interest in Lilli's work over the

9

past year. There had been an illustrated article in one of the Sunday newspaper colour magazines. A large-format colour paperback, *The Paintings of Lilli Danielsohn*, one of a series of art books, had been published some months earlier, and there had been new editions of several of her books. Next year, another firm was producing Lilli Danielsohn greetings-cards and posters, and there would be a Lilli Danielsohn calendar.

It was part of a fashion at this time, a nostalgic return to a rural past. In clothes, interior design, food, the ideal seemed to be a recreation of an idealised country cottage: tiny floral designs, simple colours, uncluttered interiors. There was a retreat from the present into the childhoods of another age, the illustrations from Victorian and Edwardian children's books.

Safe inside the ordered silence, people seemed to believe that the world beyond the window-panes would be sunfilled corn-fields, empty of all but birdsong.

Two

Fitcher's Bird was the first story from the Brothers Grimm to be illustrated by Lilli Danielsohn. *Fitcher's Bird and Other Stories* was published by the Ullstein Publishing Company in Berlin in 1929, the same year as *Emil and the Detectives* was published for the first time.

Once there was a magician who could assume the appearance of an ordinary poor man. In this form he begged from door to door, and took away pretty girls. No one knew where he took them, or what happened to them. They were never seen again.

One day he knocked on the door of a man who had three pretty young daughters. He looked exactly like a poor old beggar, with a basket on his back, as if to carry away any food or other gifts given to him. He begged for just a tiny bite of food, and the eldest daughter, moved for pity, came out to give him a piece of bread. He touched her once, gently, and she was compelled to climb into his basket. At once he sped away like the wind, leaving no tracks, and took her into the heart of a dark pathless forest, where his house was hidden.

It was a lovely house, and he surrounded her with everything she desired. He said, 'You will be happy with me for the rest of your days, my love, for I have given you everything you can ever wish for.'

Seven days later he said to her, 'I must go on a journey, and leave you by yourself for a few days. Here are all the keys

11

of the house. You may go anywhere in the house, and look at everything there is, but you must not go into one room, the room which is opened by this little key. If you go into this room, you will die, my love.'

He also gave her a white egg, and said, 'You must also protect this egg very carefully for me. You must carry it around with you at all times, for grave misfortune would result if you were to lose it.'

He gave her the keys and the egg, and she promised to follow his instructions exactly. She watched him leave, and then began to explore the house, from room to room, from the cellars to the attic, looking closely at everything. The house was rich with silver and gold, and as she walked through the gleaming quiet rooms she thought that she had never seen such beauty.

Finally, she came to the forbidden door of the room she must not enter. She thought she would just walk past it, but she began to wonder what was behind that door. It was a door like any other door. She examined the little key carefully. It was a key like any other key. She put the key in the keyhole, turned it only a little, and the door was open.

What did she see inside that room?

An enormous bloody bowl stood in the middle of the room, piled with the dead bodies of human beings, hacked to pieces. Beside the bowl was a wooden chopping-block, and an axe which gleamed as brightly as the gold had done. She was so terrified that she let the egg fall from her hand into the blood-filled bowl. She quickly pulled it out, and tried to wipe the blood off with the corner of her dress, but the blood would not be removed. All day she washed and scrubbed, but the blood remained on the egg.

After seven days, the magician returned from his journey, and the first thing he did was to ask for the keys and the egg. She gave them to him, but she was trembling, and there were tears in her eyes. He saw immediately, by the bloodstains, that she had been in the forbidden room.

'You have been into the forbidden room against my will,'

12

he said quietly. 'Now you shall go back into it against your own will. Your life is over.' Calmly, he threw her to the floor, dragged her by her long hair, cut her head off on the wooden chopping-block, and hacked her body to pieces, so that her blood ran along the ground. Then he threw the pieces of her body into the bowl with all the others.

'Now I will go for the second daughter,' said the magician, and again he went to the house in the form of a poor old beggar, and begged for just a tiny bite of food. The second daughter, moved for pity, came out to give him a piece of bread, and he caught her as he had caught the first, by touching her once, gently, and then carrying her away.

The same thing happened to her as had happened to her sister.

She was left with the keys and the egg, and opened the door of the forbidden room. She paid for it with her life when the magician returned.

The magician then went and brought the third daughter.

Seven days later he said to her, 'I must go on a journey, and leave you by yourself for a few days.' He gave her the keys and the egg, and gave her the same instructions as he had given her two sisters.

The third daughter was thoughtful and intelligent. When the magician had gone, she hid the egg away very carefully, and then began to explore the house. Finally, she opened the door of the forbidden room.

What did she see inside that room?

Both her beloved sisters lay heaped there in the bloody bowl, murdered, and hacked to pieces. Weeping, she began to gather the pieces of their bodies together, and lay them out in order on the floor: the head, the body, the arms, and the legs. When all the pieces were lying together, they began to move, and the bodies were made whole again. The two sisters opened their eyes, and were alive once more. They kissed and embraced each other very lovingly.

After seven days, the magician returned from his journey, and the first thing he did was to ask for the keys and the egg.

13

There was no trace of any bloodstains on the egg, and he said, 'You have passed my test. You shall be my bride.'

He no longer had any power over her, and had to do whatever she told him.

'I shall be your bride,' she said, 'but you must first take a gift of gold to my father and mother, and carry it yourself upon your back in your basket. I will remain here, and prepare our wedding-feast.'

She ran to her sisters, whom she had hidden away in a little secret chamber, and said, 'The time has come when you can be saved. The magician himself will carry you home again, but as soon as you are home, send help to save me.'

She hid both her sisters in the basket, and covered them over with gold, so that they were quite hidden. She then called for the magician, and said to him, 'Here is the gold you are to take to my father and mother. Carry the basket to them. I shall be looking after you through my little window, and I shall see if you stop on the way to sit and rest.'

The magician pulled the basket on to his back, and began to walk away with it through the forest, though it weighed him down so heavily that the sweat poured from him. After a time, he was so tired that he sat down, and wished to rest, but as soon as he did this, one of the sisters in the basket cried out, 'I am looking through my little window, and I can see that you have stopped. You must go on again at once.'

He thought it was his bride who was talking to him, got to his feet, and began to walk on.

He had walked a little further, when he felt tired again, and sat down, but the other sister immediately cried out, 'I am looking through my little window, and I can see that you have stopped. You must go on again at once.'

Every time he paused, or tried to sit down, the sisters cried this out, and he was compelled to move onwards. Finally, groaning and breathless, he arrived at the parents' house, with the gold, and the two sisters.

In the house in the forest, the magician's bride prepared the wedding-feast, and sent invitations to all the magician's friends.

14

Then she took a skull with its grinning teeth, put rich jewellery around it, flowers in its eye-sockets, and decked it with a garland, and carried it upstairs to her little window, so that it looked as if it were looking out. Then she cut open the feather-bed, covered herself in honey, and rolled herself in the feathers until she looked like a strange and wonderful bird, and could not be recognised.

As she walked away from the house and through the forest, she met the magician's friends on their way to the wedding-feast. They asked her:

'Fitcher's bird, how did you come to be here?'

'I have come from Fitcher's house, quite near.'

'Where is the young bride, and what is she doing?'

'From cellar to attic all's sparkling and new,

And from her little window she's looking at you.'

Further along in the forest she met the magician, who was coming slowly back from her parents' house. He asked her the same questions as the others:

'Fitcher's bird, how did you come to be here?'

'I have come from Fitcher's house, quite near.'

'Where is the young bride, and what is she doing?'

'From cellar to attic all's sparkling and new,

And from her little window she's looking at you.'

The magician looked up, and saw the disguised skull in the window. He thought it was his bride, and called up to her. Then he and all his friends went into the house for the wedding-feast.

At this moment, the brothers and all the relatives of the bride arrived, sent to save her by her sisters. They locked all the doors of the house, and closed all the shutters, so that no one could escape, and set fire to it.

The magician, and all his friends, perished in the flames.

Three

Lilli Danielsohn's illustration for *Fitcher's Bird* was a water-colour, a double-page spread of a quiet interior flooded with warm light, a meticulous representation of a middle-class German bedroom in the late 1920s. On the extreme right of the picture, a beautiful dark-haired girl, the second sister, was beginning to open a door set into the bedroom wall. The curtains over the window were about to billow outwards into the room as the door opened. Plants on the window-ledge, a carved table, an oil-lamp, the individual threads in a woven bed-cover.

Beyond the bedroom door, unseen and unrecorded, was the mutilated body of her murdered sister. No blood seeped beneath the door into the image of domestic peace. In her left hand the girl held the fragile egg, which, when stained with blood, would mean that her life was over. Her face, in intense close-up, the eyes very large, did not look towards the forbidden room, but gazed out of the picture, towards the onlooker. She was very young.

After he had poured the boiling water into the tea-pot, he sat down to wait for a while before pouring out the tea.

The Kate Greenaway playing-cards Mum had fixed on the fridge-door were still there. The six of diamonds had a picture of three little boys at the entrance to a church-yard. *We're all jolly boys, and we're coming with a noise.* Mum. It was Jo who had started calling her that. When she was alive they had

16

called her Margaret, as they had been brought up to call all adults by their Christian names.

He stared at the painted enamel eggs in the egg-cups on the pine dresser as he poured milk, and then tea, into Lilli's tea-cup, and poured out some orange-juice for Matthias. The nearest one to him was of two boys in sailor-suits, carrying a model yacht.

He carried the cup and the orange-juice through into the sun-lounge. The sun-lounge ran the full length of the back of theirs and Lilli's house, and their kitchen and dining-room both opened into it. He liked to hear the rain rattling against the glass roof. His parents had always referred to it as the sun-lounge – ludicrous though that term was on a day like this one – perhaps thinking that the word 'conservatory' had grandiose overtones, appropriate though it might be in an Edwardian house. Jo, more accurately, called it the grot-hole. The floor was littered with Matthias's toys.

He pushed his way through carefully, bricks and model cars rattling across the tiles. He noticed a model soldier stuck in the soil of a plantpot near Baskerville's basket and wondered how it had got there. They had never been allowed toy guns, or any toys connected with war or war-games.

He peered through the glass, masking his eyes against the reflected light. He saw a torch approaching through the grave-stones in the burial-ground, and the pointed hood of Jo's anorak as he skipped exaggeratedly along the path.

The connecting door between the two houses was in the sun-lounge, and he walked through into Lilli's house. The floor of her sun-lounge was equally cluttered.

Matthias, his three-year-old youngest brother was there, kneeling on a chair up against the table near Lilli's hand-loom, leaning over a painting with immense concentration. His nose was dull green with dried paint. He was three years old, three feet high, and weighed three stone, a pleasing symmetry which Jo regarded as a strong argument against metrication.

The smell of cooking came through the open door from the kitchen.

'How's Horrible Horace?' Corrie asked, handing him the orange-juice. It was in a covered tumbler, with a little raised rim to drink from. He liked the special things made for small children.

Matthias leaned back against his chair, and surveyed the over-all effect of his painting, like an artist checking his perspective, and then, very seriously, as though he were a French general bestowing an honour, he kissed Corrie on the cheek, to thank him for the orange-juice. He was very lavish with his kisses with people he knew well.

'I'm not Horrible Horace!' he said.

'Murderous Matty? What have you done with my grand-mother?'

'Making a German Christmas! I'm going to stay up late tonight!'

Matthias's voice always became very high and shrill when he was excited or amused.

'I bet you've eaten her. I can see a bit of her shoe in your teeth.'

'What big teeth you've got!' Matthias shouted, adding, a moment later, 'I'm not hungry.'

Corrie walked round to look at Matthias's painting. There was a preponderance of green, applied in thick vertical strokes, and a large red blob at one side.

'What is it a picture of?' he asked.

'A havverglumpus,' Matthias replied, with withering contempt. At least Corrie had looked at the picture the right way up this time.

He looked for somewhere safe to put Lilli's cup of tea, away from Matthias's paint-brushes. He noticed that her easel was out, at the edge of the sun-lounge along from the loom, and wondered why Matthias wasn't using that. He eventually placed the cup on the bench in front of the loom.

This was the day when, in term-time, he and Jo came after school to have tea with Lilli. It was a tradition that had started some months ago, on a day free of orchestra practice and other school commitments, and they had carried it through into the

18

holidays. Lilli would set out the table in the dining-room with flowers, a hand-woven cloth, and her best china, and they would spend an hour or so talking about the week at school, playing some of the new pieces they had learned on their instruments. He had grown to need those times with Lilli. Today they had suspended the custom, as Lilli was preparing the dining-room for her Christmas, but he had promised to bring her some tea.

He went further along the sun-lounge, and went through the door into the living-room. Lilli's house still had two separate rooms downstairs, the dining-room at the front, facing out onto Dunwich Green, and the living-room at the back. In their house the two rooms had been knocked into one, and they had one long room running the full depth of the house, with an arch in the middle where there had once been a wall. Lilli's living-room was still waiting to be redecorated, bare and echoing, like a room in an empty house, the floorboards uncarpeted, and the furniture under dustcovers.

He went through into the hall, passed the dining-room door, and picked up the evening-paper from the floor beneath the letterbox. *Carols at Siege School*. The subheadings in the report stood out. *Politics. Terrorists. Hostages. Demands.* It seemed as good a summary as he had ever read of modern life in Western Europe.

He knocked on the dining-room door.

'Tea is served, modom.'

'Thank you, my good man,' Lilli said, as she came out, using the phrase that Jo normally used when he did something for him.

He offered her his arm, and they went through the kitchen into the sun-lounge. Matthias sat sucking at the orange-juice, as though he were plugged into the tumbler. He was always entirely self-absorbed when he was dealing with food or drink.

The sound of the rain on the sun-lounge roof was louder than it had been all afternoon. There was going to be a carol-service round the tree on Dunwich Green at eight-thirty. Jo was going to sing a solo.

'We need snow for tonight, not rain,' he said to Lilli. 'The more it snows . . .'

'Tiddely-pom!' Matthias said. He had finished his orange-juice.

'We can't have an Outdoor Hum for Snowy Weather when it's raining.'

'And when we're indoors,' Lilli added.

'I expect we'll get all the snow at Easter.'

There had been snow on the ground when Mum had been buried.

He looked across at Lilli. She was sitting on the bench in front of the loom, holding her cup and saucer in one hand. There was a great quality of stillness about her. He had talked to her about most things, sometimes when Jo was not there, but he could not talk to her about what he had found in the inner room of The Ferry House.

He leaned across Matthias, and held his painting up towards Lilli.

'What's this a picture of?'

'A havverglumpus, of course,' she said, as if amazed that he hadn't known.

'Of *course*!' Matthias repeated, looking at Corrie with great scorn.

He climbed down from his chair, and went across to Lilli, then stood with his legs apart, and his arms raised away from his sides, looking into the distance. Corrie looked at him, puzzled.

'Have you wet yourself?' he asked eventually, after Matthias had held the pose for some time.

'No! I'm standing like Rupert the Bear.'

He was still standing like Rupert the Bear, and shrieking, 'Splishity-Splash!' when he went back into Tennyson's, their house, closing the connecting door between them.

His other little brother was in the kitchen, pouring out two mugs of tea. He was wearing his shiny green anorak with the hood up, dripping slightly, and green wellingtons. Wet footprints led through from the sun-lounge, in which Basker-

20

ville, their elderly Golden Labrador, was a wet panting heap.

Jo pushed a mug of tea across to him.

'How now, boy!' Corrie said.

'I am like you, they say.'

'Why, there's some comfort.'

Corrie and Jo regularly addressed each other through quotations, belabouring each other with their erudition. Jo, who was eleven, was quite capable of keeping up with his older brother. Corrie had written the music for the school production of *The Winter's Tale*, performed a fortnight before the end of term, and they were still quoting that to each other. Jo had played the little boy Mamillius, and, in the final scene of the play – offstage, unseen, dead sixteen years – he had sung a song written by Corrie, *'Tis time, descend, be stone no more*, the music heard as Hermione, Mamillius's mother, stepped back into life to be reunited with her husband Leontes. He had a beautiful singing voice.

'How's Lilli?' he asked.

'All prepared. Six o'clock.'

He looked at the pointed hood, and Jo's sharp-featured face.

'You look just like a garden gnome dressed like that,' he said.

'That's right,' Jo answered, swinging his legs round. 'I'm the National Elf.'

He kicked his wellingtons off, hung his anorak on one of the hooks beside the door in the sun-lounge, and began to unwind his long scarf round and round his head.

'The Ideal Gnome!'

He reached up for a biscuit from the tin with the reproduction Victorian design for Colman's mustard, and then began to entrechat about the kitchen, jumping up and down and trying to stand on tip-toe, making extravagant sweeping arm-movements, pirouetting through into the living-room. The paintings from school pinned on the family notice-board in the kitchen flapped as he went past.

'Curse this truss,' he said eventually, and sat down, switching on the television.

He picked up the atlas that Corrie had been resting his music

21

notebook on, and took out the pieces of the cut-up *Fitcher's Bird* illustration, sliding them into place. In an early lesson with Lilli, months ago, he had slit the reproduction from one of his copies of the paperback, and cut it up into thirty pieces to make a simple jigsaw for her to put back together again.

'*The heart of a dark pathless forest,*' he quoted, as Corrie sat down beside him, carrying his mug of tea. They were both dressed in their best clothes, ready for the German Christmas, wanting to do the right thing for what Lilli had been planning.

As the television picture appeared, a photograph of a blood-stained body filled the screen. The school siege was the main news again. The German terrorists had killed a woman who had tried to move up towards the school, the mother of one of the children. It was 5.15, and the special news bulletin for children was just beginning.

Jo leaned forward, and then jumped up to walk back through into the sun-lounge. Corrie heard the clicking of Baskerville's nails as he slid around the tiles, and the occasional clatter as he ploughed through the heaped toys.

'We will execute all those who try to approach too near us,' the Red Phoenix terrorists had announced. 'We will make no concessions whatsoever.'

He looked down at his tea. It was in a Peter Rabbit mug. Peter's mother was speaking to her children. He wondered whether Jo's dislike of Mr McGregor in school was based upon a memory from early childhood.

Jo was thinking about Mum again. He did his daft things, and made his quick comments as much as he ever did, but he did them automatically, his voice quite separate from the rest of him. He had recently reverted to the disturbed pattern of sleep he had had after Mum's death. For two months afterwards he had had nightmares, and Dr Disken had put him on to some tablets to help him sleep. Last night Corrie had woken up at three o'clock and gone to the lavatory, and the light had been on in Jo's room. He had gone into his room, but Jo had been asleep, and he had left again after switching

22

off the light – a little nursery night-light that Jo had had since he was three.

'Jo!' he called, as the news came to an end. 'Charlie Brown.'

'Good grief!' came from the sun-lounge in a chirpy small American boy's voice, but the cartoon had been started for some time before he came back into the living-room.

Small American children, serious and absorbed as any children in a Breughel painting, were discussing tactics in a baseball game they were about to play. Jo settled back, his head down at the base of the chesterfield, his feet, higher than his head, resting on top of a newly-towelled and dishevelled Baskerville, who accepted his role as footstool with the weary resignation sometimes registered by Snoopy. Jo laughed frequently, a high breathless chuckle, identical to the way in which Corrie laughed.

After the programme finished, there would be a five-minute programme for very young children, just before their bed-time, though he and Jo always watched it, usually claiming they were only watching it because Matthias was there. He would be watching it next-door with Lilli. The current series was based upon the Winnie the Pooh stories. Jo still had a battered Winnie the Pooh that Mum had made for him. He called it his Linus's blanket. After this there would be the early evening news, and the picture of the murdered woman would fill the screen again.

Colour television had brought the colour of blood into the living-room. There was no dignity or privacy in death any more. Victims of road-accidents or air-disasters, murder or terrorism, had photographs of their destroyed bodies in newspapers or on television, to be looked at by strangers.

We will execute all those who try to approach too near us. We will make no concessions whatsoever. The name of Rome airport had made him see tall enigmatically-smiling figures emerging from shadows, looking down over Mum's body lying on the bloodstained floor, pointing fingers, a ruinous Last Supper, note-books filled with mirror-writing, diagrams of unborn children in the womb. If they had had a television-set

23

nine months ago, perhaps they would have switched it on one evening to watch Piglet going in search of a Heffalump, and seen the body of their murdered mother lying awkwardly amidst broken glass on the marble floor of an airport lounge. She would have been wearing her green coat.

They had been sheltered within that quiet house, behind the walls which surrounded the school, and the outside world had been far away. The television was less than two months old. Things had happened far off, on the rim of a distant world, too far away ever to enter their quietude.

He picked up the two empty mugs and walked through into the kitchen.

Beside the sink was *The Wind in the Willows* calendar that Mum had bought last Christmas. It would be time to take it down soon. Christmas Day was circled, and the 28th of December, his birthday.

The December E. H. Shepard illustration was of the carol-singers outside Mole End. Mole was at the door, holding a candle, looking out at the group of tiny singing field-mice. It was a picture that seemed to him, like Lilli's illustrations, to carry an acute sense of sadness and melancholy behind it, a feeling of loss, and time passing. Perhaps it was just him, thinking of looking at the same illustration in the book when he was little, and Mum reading it to him. At nearly sixteen, watching small children at play, he sometimes felt that he would never feel as old again as he felt at those moments. He had a copy of *The Wind in the Willows* and other children's books near his bed, as carefully hidden as if they were pornography.

Above the illustration was the description of the carol-singers from the novel. *In the fore-court, lit by the dim rays of a horn lantern, some eight or ten little field-mice stood in a semi-circle, red worsted comforters round their throats, their fore-paws thrust deep into their pockets, their feet jogging for warmth. With bright beady eyes they glanced shyly at each other, sniggering a little, sniffing and applying coat-sleeves a good deal.*

He ran the hot water into the mugs, wiping round the inside

24

with the cloth. He remembered a phrase from a little further on in the novel, just before the words of the carol: *shrill little voices*. He could still hear the rain beating against the glass roof of the sun-lounge.

London, N16.
30th March 1938.

Dear Mr High,

Miss Greif told me that you will accept my boy Walter who has been at school in Berlin in your school at once at the much reduced fee of £55. I do not know how to thank you for your kindness. As I was well-off until only a short time ago it was hard for me to ask you to moderate the school fees. Miss Greif will have told you that I was a musician in Germany, and as I am Jewish I have lost every means of earning a livelihood there. I have been here in England trying to begin a new existence. My wife and two daughters are still in Germany waiting for the time when I shall be able to support them here, and they can join me and be safe. I hope this time comes soon. Mrs Werth, Dr phil., was a lecturer and has now no more right to teach in Germany.

My son will arrive in London this week. I have not seen him for a year, and would like to have him with me for two days, if you will allow me. Please do not send my bill to my wife in Berlin, because of the special circumstances in Germany. She cannot write to you from Berlin such as she wants to.

With great thankfulness,
Leon Werth.

He heard the high urgent signature tune of the news beginning in the living-room, and then the television was switched off, and all the living-room lights.

Jo came into the kitchen, and walked through into the sun-lounge.

'Hello,' he said to Cyril, the umbrella plant on the desk. 'It is I, Johann. Are you pleased to see me?'

He began to slide on the tiles, using his stockinged feet.

'Ready for the carol service, Jo?'

Jo immediately assumed a coy expression, folded his hands in front of him, and began to sing in a very high-pitched voice.

> 'Once in royal David's city
> Stood a lowly cattle shed,
> Where a mother laid her baby
> In a manger for his bed:
> Mary was that mother mild,
> Jesus Christ her little child.'

'You're not singing that!'

Jo shook his head.

'No. And not like that either.'

He sat on the floor, and began to put his shoes on.

'Do you know you're going mouldy, Corrie? I've tactfully refrained from mentioning it so far, knowing how sensitive you are about your appearance. One doesn't wish to cause embarrassment.'

Corrie rubbed his hand across his face, and looked at the powdery green streaks from Matthias's poster-paint.

'Just thought I'd mention it,' Jo said.

'We were *always* singing that carol in junior school,' he said. '*Away in a Manger. We Three Kings. While Shepherds Watched.* Do you remember hymn-singing in junior school?'

'*Daisies Are Our Silver. All things bright and beautiful. Little drops of water.* "Please, miss, he had his eyes open during the prayer." Mrs Bradbury could never grasp the fact that if someone saw you with your eyes open, he must have had his eyes open as well.'

'I remember you shoving your head up where the glove compartment used to be in that abandoned car, and pretending to be the radio.'

'Hi there, all you listeners in wonderful radio-land.'

'You never liked the Romans in Miss Pinion's history lessons, because they all went to the lavatory together.'

'Filthy beasts!'

Jo was wandering restlessly about the sun-lounge, touching at the window-frames.

'I wish I'd seen Matthias in that nativity play.'

'I giggle just thinking about it.'

During the previous week Matthias had spoken of nothing but the nativity play which his play-school had been rehearsing to perform before an audience of mothers and grandparents. He had told them all about it. He was the Gold king, and the two other kings were called Frankenstein and Mirth. Frankenstein wouldn't kneel down, and, at the actual performance, Joseph's beard had come off, and he had dropped baby Jesus off the end of the stage. He had bounced two feet into the air, and Guy Richens' grandmother had laughed so much that she had fallen backwards off a bench, and everyone had seen her knickers. Jo had enjoyed hearing that bit.

There was a pause.

Jo moved across towards Corrie, and sat down on the floor near Baskerville, scratching his head. He looked up at Corrie, his face serious.

'Why can't Pieter be here with us for Christmas?'

Their father had flown to the United States a week earlier.

'He explained to us all about that, Jo. He's got a phone-call booked to talk to us tonight, hasn't he?'

'Massachusetts,' Jo whispered, as though speaking an incantation. 'Remember Lilli telling us that, in Germany, Christmas Eve is a time when the close family are alone together?'

'Think of those children in Berlin.'

In the silence that followed, all the lights suddenly went out. The kitchen clock began to chime six o'clock, and then, on the other side of the house, the school clock above the main building began to chime, the deep notes echoing out across the Green. They were enclosed in a faintly-gleaming glass box, watery shadows streaming down, as if they were below the

27

surface of deep water, drawn down by the Nixie of the Mill-Pond.

On Lilli's side of the sun-lounge there was a faint subdued glow, splintered by the frosted glass of the connecting door. As they watched, Jo still sitting on the floor, the glow grew in intensity, and swaying, liquescent light came nearer. The door opened, and Lilli stood in the doorway, holding a candlestick in each hand. Illuminated by the soft, flickering light, her face intent, she was like a figure in a Gerrit van Honthorst nativity scene. Her hair was drawn back from her face, and she was wearing a simple floor-length dress.

Looking straight ahead of her, she began to make a formal little speech, her face impassive.

'A German Christmas is a very special time. Watch Night, *Weihnachten*, is associated with magical revelations. Mountains open and reveal their hoards of precious stones, church bells ring out from cities at the bottom of the sea, trees burst into blossom and fruit, the sun jumps thrice for joy, and the pure in heart can understand the language of animals.'

She paused, and then raised her voice, calling out loudly.

'Magical revelations!'

From an inner room in Lilli's house, a hand-bell began to ring, a high silvery sound.

'Come,' Lilli said, standing aside from the door, smiling, beckoning them towards her, giving each of them a candlestick, placing her arms around their shoulders, 'Come inside.'

Four

They followed Lilli through the darkened living-room, where Matthias was standing, immensely excited, ringing a little silver bell, and all of them moved slowly into the unlit hallway at the foot of the stairs, to wait outside the dining-room. The candles swayed in the cool currents of air, and, as they stood there, they could see the shape of the dining-room door outlined in a rippling light that shone through the gaps between the door and the frame from inside the dining-room.

'This is the special room that no one has been allowed into,' Lilli said. 'Why did the bell ring?'

'Father Christmas has just gone!' Matthias shouted, very shrill, the bell ringing erratically as he jumped up and down.

'And what has he left for us in this room?'

The words were like a catechism.

'Christmas presents, and the tree, the tree!'

Matthias was in an ecstasy of expectancy.

'Open the door, Matty.'

Lilli gave a small, conspiratorial smile to Corrie and Jo as Matthias put his hand on the door-knob, hesitated rather nervously, looked round to see that they were still with him, and then pushed it hard so that it swung completely open.

There was a squeal from Matthias.

The whole room was green and silver, lit only by the glow of scores of candles. The tree was the only decoration, dominating the whole room, up to the height of the ceiling in the corner near the window, glittering with strands of silver hanging down from every branch, and, for a moment, with the current of air gusting in as the door opened, and the heat and glow as they entered, the birthday-cake smell of burning candles, the whole tree, and the room, seemed to sway away and then back towards them as the shadows shifted. Candles covered the tree, and lined the dining-table; and Lilli's glazed paintings, lining the walls in the room, reflected back and multiplied the images of hundreds of candle-flames, hovering in the air about them like bright fluttering wings. From the glass of every painting, from the polished wooden frames, from every reflective surface in the room – the face of the clock, the glasses and cutlery on the table, the metallic paper around the presents on the low tables in the bay of the window – light danced and pulsated, as if they were in a small and brilliantly-lit church. Outside, in the cold and wet of the winter evening, the coloured bulbs on the bare branches of the horse-chestnut tree in the middle of Dunwich Green looked wan and distant, pale beyond the reflected glow in the dark glass of the window.

They were like some miniature religious procession as they moved into the room, moving towards the altar for some service of memorial. As formally as she had made her little speech in the sun-lounge, Lilli kissed each of them in turn as they stood around the table in the candlelight.

'This year we sit at the table and think of the members of our family who are not with us,' Lilli said, quietly. Corrie glanced at Jo. They stood in silence for a moment with their heads bowed, and then sat down.

Meissen china plates – he had only seen them once before – lined the centre of the table, filled with fruit, nuts and raisins, sweets, ribbons, tiny richly-decorated spiced biscuits in ornate moulded shapes, hearts and diamonds, candied lemon and orange, iced stars with cherries, all beautifully arranged, and, as the centrepiece of the whole table, there was an elaborate and minutely-detailed Hansel and Gretel gingerbread house, like the nightlight that Jo had in his bedroom. Steep-roofed, its roof covered with little twisted biscuits covered in hundreds and thousands, icing like snow dripping down from the over-hanging eaves, its door partly open, it stood beneath the candles like the cottage beneath the trees in the heart of the forest, waiting for the approach of the abandoned children.

'Beside a dark pathless forest there lived a poor woodcutter with his second wife and his two children, a little boy and a little girl,' Corrie said, looking at the gingerbread house.

'The boy was called Hansel, and the girl . . .' Lilli paused, looking at Matthias.

'Gretel!' Matthias shouted. He looked across at Corrie. 'I *do* feel hungry now. It's lovely, Lilli. It's lovely. I'm going to eat *everything*!'

He took his eating very seriously. You could take Baskerville's bowl away from him when he was eating, and he would only look very sad and miserable, but make no objection. Matthias bashed people with his spoon.

Jo started to speak, Lilli smiled, and then everyone was talking, and the muted solemnity of the beginning – an Easter mood, a Good Friday mood – became animated and lively, and Lilli – after talking with them – went back out of the room towards the kitchen, to bring in the first course of the Christmas meal.

As the meal continued, the unfamiliar weight of the silver cutlery in his hands, Corrie felt sure that Lilli, with her German Christmas, was not recreating something she had herself once experienced, an expatriate, after many years, feeding the nostalgia for a ceremony in which she had once taken part. The speech in the sun-lounge had not been her words: she had been quoting something she had read, and all he saw around him, carefully and beautifully contrived, was as novel to her as it was to them, possibly inaccurate, a creation from books and research, not from memory. Christmas was a feast she would never have kept when she was in Germany, because Christmas was not a Jewish festival.

He had a secret, sort of, about himself.

Like Nikolaus Mittler and his big brother, like Leon Werth

31

and his family, he was Jewish, and he had not known it until two years ago. As Lilli was Jewish, then, by the rulings of Germany in the 1930s, he himself – Gentile and uncircumcised – was also Jewish, a Mischling, Second Degree, a child with one Jewish grandparent. It was something inside himself, something in his blood. Wasn't descent through the female line in Jewish law?

It had been Christmas when he found out about Lilli Danielsohn, two years ago. The name had been a strange one to him, an unfamiliar disguise in someone he had known all his life. To him, his grandmother had always been Lilli, and, sometimes, when he wrote to her to thank her for presents at Christmas, or on his birthday, she was Lilli Meeuwissen when he addressed the envelope, someone with the same surname as himself. Her German accent was just the way she spoke.

Lilli had never spoken a word about her past, her life in Germany, her family, like the girl bound to silence in *The Six Swans*, and her books and paintings had remained locked away, from herself, and from everyone else. Four years ago, Grandpa Michael had died, and Lilli had left The Dutch House, where they had lived in Dorset, and moved to London. In London, living alone, her husband dead, she had begun to look at the paintings again for the first time in forty years.

At Christmas, two years ago, they had gone to see her. She had changed – become very quiet and introspective – not the seemingly stern and commanding woman he had always known – and the little house had seemed bare, a place without memories, as if she had no past she could place around her, but, on the evening of the first Sunday of their stay in London he had found out about Lilli Danielsohn when they had been talking around the fire. The things she had not spoken about for all those years were said, a decision she had come to before they arrived. It was something she had wanted to talk about.

When she married Grandpa in 1939 she had been a refugee from Germany: his parents had known this much, though he and Jo had not. When she had left the country in 1938, to arrive alone and unknown in England, she had been famous throughout Germany as an artist. Her first book – *Kinder-stimmen* – a series of illustrations for German poems about childhood had been published, in Berlin, by Ullstein, in 1924, in the same week as *When We Were Very Young* was first published in London. Her work had met with increasing success in the late 1920s and early 1930s, until, in 1933, the Nazis had come to power. Copies of her books had been burned by the Nazis in Berlin in 1933, in Unter den Linden, between the Opera House and the University. The children's stories had gone up in flames, like Erich Kästner's books, with the works of Freud, Marx, Mann, Heine, and all the others, because she and all her family were Jewish. She had been unable to have any more of her work published.

That evening, hesitant and shy, she had taken her paintings out of the drawer in the roll-top desk where she had kept them locked up for all those years, unglazed, loose in cardboard folders, and shown them to them. His parents had never known that she had been an artist. Since she left Germany, she had never painted again.

He would never forget that first evening with Lilli Daniel-sohn, and his first sight of all the paintings he now knew so well, all around him on the walls of the dining-room. That evening in London she had given each of them one of her original water-colours for a Grimm's fairy-story as a Christmas present. It was then that he had been given his illustration for *Hansel and Gretel*, the painting beside his bed that he had studied for two years. It had been the first of her paintings that he had seen, and he had thought it very beautiful. It was the loveliest present he had ever had.

She had embraced them all when they had left to return to Southwold.

They had visited her again in the summer, and she had seemed a lot older.

He had seen her one evening, thinking she was unobserved, walking about the small garden like a personification of Sorrow in a morality play, bent over, walking up and down as the light began to fail. He had been afraid to approach, shrank

33

from touching, a deep and private inner source of grief, that numbed and frozen face that looked as if it had been exposed to intense and prolonged cold. Seeing her like this, he had thought of someone carrying and shielding a flickering candle in a windswept corridor. Thoughts in her head, like candles on a child's birthday cake, dipped and bent, but never flickered out into darkness. The small intense flames were always there. Her eyes had had the blind unfocused stare of someone who had gazed too intently into the candle-flame, and who carried a dark shadow impressed deep inside her eye, burned in by too intense a light.

Several months later, she had suffered her stroke, and, after some time in hospital, Pieter had brought her from London to live next-door to them, with the connecting door between the two houses, and the months of recovery and teaching had started, and he had come to know someone new, a Lilli who was not the woman in the bare house or the dark garden.

In novels, particularly in Victorian novels, the author invented a complete family history for his characters, and, as the reader, one could know more about the histories of these fictitious families than one knew about one's own family history: this, he supposed, was part of the pleasures of fiction. What had struck him as slightly wrong was that the characters always seemed to possess an awareness of every detail of their family history – unless a startling discovery were a major part of the plot – feeling themselves firmly placed in a structured and predictable family-tree. His life had been lived with blanks and absences, emptinesses that he had been too uninformed or too reticent to find out about.

Discovering his Jewishness – it couldn't be denied, could it? – he felt as though he had opened some forbidden door, and made some shocking discovery which overturned all the certainties in his life. He felt as though he had suddenly discovered that he had been adopted, and that all his assumptions about his parentage, all his beliefs about who he was, were completely false. He had no concrete dogma to hold on to, no self-protecting litany to chant like the song of the bird in *The Juniper Tree*. It had sounded so odd when Lilli had spoken about marrying Grandpa Michael and 'becoming a Christian'. He knew hardly anything about the Jewish religion. It was something he had never talked about with anyone. He had gone with Cato once in the summer holidays to a demonstration outside the Soviet Embassy against the treatment of a Jewish dissident, but he had felt quite separate from all those angry young people, who seemed sure of who they were and what they wanted. He had been a little bit frightened.

In Lilli's house in London, amongst her many books, there had been a copy of *The Children's Haggadah*, a book published in 1937, which he had looked at, curious and confused, in the days after that Sunday evening, to try and learn something about the Jewish religion, feeling as though he were reading about an invented religion in a fictitious world, a Rousseau, a Middle Earth, a Narnia, or an Earthsea. The book read from back to front, and on the back cover was a picture of a small child in a skull-cap lying asleep in bed, clutching the book in his arms. Inside, little pieces of card could be pulled from side to side to make the pictures move: the baby Moses floated down the Nile in his basket, the Egyptian army sank beneath the sea. *On the evening before the eve of Passover, the father of the family goes into every room of his house to see whether all leavened food has been cleared away. It is customary to place small pieces of bread in every room, and the father collects them carefully by the light of a candle. These are burned on the following morning soon after breakfast.*

If he had discovered that he were a Roman Catholic, and had not known it, he would have felt the same suffocating approach of things of which he knew little: candles, rosaries, rich vestments, and confessions of one's most secret thoughts to an unknown man. But he had been in a Catholic church, fearful of being approached by a priest or nun who would assume he knew all about the mysteries of their faith. He had never been inside a synagogue. He had seen one once, from a car, and it had seemed an intensely-enclosed and private place, a windowless façade, inward-looking, a place to which no strangers could ever be admitted.

The lights began to dim, like a coal fire beginning to settle. Candles began to gutter and go out, one by one, as the meal came to an end. When the candles were all out, they would begin to open their presents, opening gifts in the evening, with the birth, not waiting until the following morning, after the child had been born. He looked around at the shifting luminescence of the many candles. Wasn't there a Jewish festival called The Feast of Lights? Was it a feast of rejoicing, or a memorial for the dead? All the candles, flickering across the glass of the water-colours, the figures indistinct in the blurred air, were like the candles one lit in churches on the continent, praying in memory of those who were dead.

If there were any self-portrait in Lilli's illustrations, showing her as he had seen her that Christmas, two years ago, it was the illustration of the mother in *The Wilful Child*, the shortest story she had ever illustrated, only a third of a side long, the final illustration in the last book she had had published in Germany, at the very beginning of 1933.

It was the expression on this mother's face that he had seen on Lilli's face. The curious, ambiguous mixture of anguish and determination on the mother's face was the expression of a woman trying to will herself to creep up and smother a much-loved child who was dying painfully of a lingering illness.

Seven o'clock sounded from the school clock, clear and distinct at the front of the house, and then, a short while later, from the mechanical bells of the clock above the Dutch restaurant on the side of the Green opposite the school, followed by the chiming of the music for the folk-song *Long A-Growing*. They moved away from the table, and sat around the fire. They sat in the dimming light, a cave of chiaroscuro, like Lilli's illustration for *Snow White*, the little girl kneeling on the chair in the country cottage, reaching up towards the open window where a hand appeared, holding out half an apple

36

towards her. On the table nearest to Corrie was an oddly-shaped parcel, labelled *To Baskerville, with love from Jo*. He signed his name 'jO', with a small 'j', and a smiling face – two dots and a curve – inside a very large 'O'. There was a separate table for each person's presents.

Until the candles burned fully down, before the presents could be opened, they were to read, and play music, recite poems they had newly learned by heart. Lilli had asked him and Jo if they would do this, a week before Christmas, after Pieter had left to drive to London, the same day as the terrorists had entered the Berlin school. They were both used to performing, particularly music. Corrie had started an Elizabethan consort in school, The Elizabethan World Picture, and Pieter, Mum, he and Jo had regularly played together, for friends and relations, or by themselves, a family in a quiet room, absorbed in a piece of music together. Their instruments were ready in the room, placed there before Lilli had started to prepare it. They had practised their pieces in The Ferry House.

Lilli began by reading the story of the nativity from St Luke's gospel, words of scripture – *swaddling clothes, a multitude of the heavenly host* – that had been a part of the mind since early childhood, like some hymns, and certain poems and stories, as if they had always been there, a rhythm of sound that awoke memories in the mind of the time before the words had been understood.

When Lilli had finished reading, Jo stood up, and began to sing in his clear, pure voice, *In the bleak mid-winter*, the carol he was going to sing in the service on the Green. Lilli was not going to come out into the rain and cold, though Sal was coming round later that night, and Matthias would not have been alone in the house. Sal and Lilli would watch from the dining-room window.

Everyone applauded when he had finished, and he bowed to each of them in turn.

'Thank you,' he said. 'Unexpected and gratifying, if a little lacking in Smack.'

It was Corrie's turn now.

He brought over one of the dining-chairs, and sat down with his cello, spending a long time shifting his position, until he was completely satisfied. Jo, standing beside him, looked at him for his signal.

Corrie took a deep breath. They were going to perform one of the songs he had written for *Hansel and Gretel*. He had found the words he had set to music in *Kinderstimmen*, the final poem in the book: *Auf meines Kindes Tod*. It was by Joseph von Eichendorff, a nineteenth-century German writer. He had got Jo to learn it in the original German.

'This is especially for Lilli,' he said. 'You won't recognise the music, but I think you'll recognise the words.'

He felt very nervous of playing this is front of other people, even though they were people who had often listened to music he had written, but Lilli had given him a part of herself in giving him her painting: he would now give her a part of himself back in return, a piece of music he had written himself.

He nodded at Jo, and, bent over the cello, began to play the long piece of wordless music before the song began. At the exact moment he moved into a higher key, Jo began to sing.

> 'Von fern die Uhren schlagen,
> Es ist schon tiefe Nacht,
> Die Lampe brennt so düster,
> Dein Bettlein ist gemacht.
>
> Die Winde nur noch gehen
> Wehklagend um das Haus.
> Wir sitzen einsam drinnen
> Und lauschen oft hinaus.
>
> Es ist, als müsstest leise
> Du klopfen an die Tür . . .'

The illustration of the empty cradle was on the wall opposite them.

When he had finished playing, Corrie held his position for a moment, and then relaxed, leaning back and looking across at Lilli. She was gazing across at the painting, holding tightly on to Matthias as he sat on her knee, lying against her. She said nothing for some time, and then looked at him.

'You wrote that music, Corrie, didn't you?'

He nodded.

'I have never heard that poem as a song before, but with that music you have made it into a beautiful song. Thank you.'

After they had listened to some poetry, and Matthias had sung a song he had heard on the radio, the same line over and over again, Jo played a gavotte on his flute, composed for him by Corrie, as Matthias did one of his dances, jigging from foot to foot, and turning round and round. The last candle finally went out as Corrie was playing his cello. They listened in the darkness, in the firelight, until he had finished, and then the lights were put on, and the presents were opened.

Corrie had just finished drying the last plate, when Jo, who had finished his share of the washing-up a short while before him, reappeared in the kitchen.

'Come and listen!' he whispered, and signalled to Corrie, like a very small boy expressing urgency in an old black and white film.

Corrie moved out into Lilli's hall, closing the kitchen door behind him, moving very quietly, caught by Jo's mood. He sat down on the bottom stair, beside Jo, his feet next to some of Matthias's scattered toys. There was a little woolly bear that he remembered Mum buying him in Bamburgh when he was seven. He picked it up, and dangled it by one of its paws.

From upstairs they could hear Lilli telling Matthias the story of *The Wolf and the Seven Little Kids*. Matthias had come down, washed, and dressed for bed, when they were in the middle of doing the dishes, to kiss them both goodnight. Jo sat with his knees pulled up against his chest, and his head leaning on its side on top of them, listening very intently.

' "The seven little kids cried, 'You must show us your paws first before you can come in, so that we will know that you really are our dear kind mother.' So the wolf put his flour-covered paws in through the window, and when the little kids saw that they were white, they believed that he really was their mother, and they opened the door. And in came the wolf! They were terrified, and . . ." '

Lilli sounded quite anxious. She always read stories well.

They listened a little longer.

'Corrie, do you remember when Mum used to read me that story?'

Jo's face was turned away from Corrie, and he could not see his expression.

'Yes, I do.'

'That time when I had asthma really badly.'

' "In tears," ' Lilli was saying upstairs, ' "the mother goat called out the name of her youngest child, and a little voice said, 'Mother, dear, dear mother, I am hiding in the clock-case.' " '

Jo pushed at the bear that Corrie was holding by its front paws, until it rocked backwards and forwards.

'When we were in the dining-room, before we opened the presents . . .' Jo began. 'When we were there, performing for Lilli, it reminded me of the Victorian Evening.'

'Yes.'

'That was the last time we saw Mum, and we didn't realise.'

Jo's hair was tousled from where it had rubbed against his knees.

On the Sunday night before Mum had flown to Rome they had put on a Victorian Evening for Lilli, still suffering from the after-effects of her stroke. Pieter had driven their mother to the airport early the following morning, when he and Jo were still in bed.

Then, unexpectedly, Jo smiled.

'I will always remember that evening.'

Jo had drawn a programme for Lilli in a variety of elaborate Victorian type-styles, and they had furnished the window-bay of Lilli's dining-room like the corner of a Victorian drawing-room, carrying through the scrap-screen from their living-room, moving the chaise-lounge round, and putting Jo's model theatre

40

on a small tripod-table, and Cyril – deputising for an aspidestra – on a jardinière from the sun-lounge. Wearing Victorian clothes they had performed for an hour, with Lilli as their only audience. They had acted an extract from *Lady Audley's Secret*, with Jo, who had rapidly assumed a woman's costume, a memorable Alicia. Mum had been Lady Audley. They had read the death of Little Nell, extracts from a handbook of Victorian etiquette, *Casabianca*, *Lips that Touch Liquor Shall Never Touch Mine*, among others – and sung several Victorian songs. The one Corrie remembered best was Mum and Jo singing *Won't You Buy My Pretty Flowers?*

Upstairs, Lilli was reaching the end of the story.

' "... the heavy stones made the wolf fall into the well, and he was drowned. When the seven little kids saw what had happened, they came running up to the well and shouted for joy, 'The wicked wolf is dead! The wicked wolf is dead!' They danced around the well with their mother." '

Jo pushed at the bear again, and it fell to the floor.

He was bending down to pick it up, when the door-bell was rung, three times, in a signal they recognised.

'Sal.'

Sal had been Mum's closest friend in Southwold, and was a regular caller at both houses.

She staggered in through the door as if she had been given a violent push in the back when Corrie opened it, struggling with her umbrella and several parcels. She groaned hollowly, and leaned back against the door, as if gathering the strength to close it.

'What a night!'

She dumped the parcels into Corrie's arms, and kissed him on the cheek.

'Happy Christmas, gorgeous.'

She ran her hands through the tight curls of her newly-permed hair, shaking out the wetness, and brushed at the front of her clothing. She peered closely at Corrie's hair, assuming a scowl. She claimed to be deeply resentful of Corrie's dark

41

curly hair, a style that Sal liked, and one that she could only achieve by visits to the hairdresser's.

'You're not really letting poor little Jo sing out on the Green in this weather, are you, you rotten swine?'

'Did you call my name, belovèd?' asked Jo, standing up, and striking a dramatic pose.

'Can it be he?' Sal said, clutching her hands to her heart as she turned to face him.

'My own!' he called. 'I yearn to be with you! Clasp me to your bosom! Madden me with desire!'

They both flung their arms open, and Jo dived into Sal's arms, and she hoisted him up into the air, his feet dangling, and pressed him against her.

'My angel!'

It was a performance they regularly went through together, once in the middle of Norwich market-place when they had seen Sal there. A stall-holder had offered Jo a cauliflower to swop places with him.

'Can we tone down these scenes of unbridled passion?' Corrie asked.

'Heavens, we're observed!' said Jo, his voice rather muffled.

Lilli began to come downstairs.

'I like that new pendant you've got round your neck,' she said to Sal. It was the first time she had joined in with one of their silly sessions.

Sal started laughing, and dropped Jo.

'He's too heavy to wear for long,' Sal said. 'You've been feeding him up again.'

'We've left you a few scraps,' Corrie said. 'Mind that lump in the carpet.'

Sal stepped over Jo, and took Corrie's arm as they went through into the dining-room.

'Do you happen to have the time on you?' Corrie asked later, as they walked through Lilli's kitchen towards the sun-lounge. He had been asking Jo the time every quarter of an hour or so since Jo had unwrapped his present. Corrie had given him

42

a combined Christmas and birthday present, an expensive gift that he had been saving up for for some time: a Snoopy wristwatch, with the dog's front legs as the hands of the watch. Lugubriously, clutching a tennis-racket in one hand, he swung his arms round and round the dial.

Exaggeratedly, Jo pulled back the cuff of his shirt, and moved the wrist with the watch on up towards his face, twisting it from side to side so that the watch faced alternately towards him, and away from him.

'The time by my brand-new Snoopy watch is 8.07 precisely.'

'I say, what a spiffing watch!'

Corrie and Jo often spoke in the slang of old-fashioned school stories, assuming a painfully genteel and high-pitched accent, parodying the role assigned to them in fiction.

'Santa brought it for me. I can tell the time now!'

'How *super*!'

The lights were on again on their side of the sun-lounge, and in the kitchen. Baskerville was lying in his basket beside the desk with an expression of utter abandonment and desolation on his face. He lumbered heavily to his feet as they came in, looking guardedly pleased.

Jo waved the parcel he had brought through from Lilli's, and began to circle around Baskerville.

'I've got a prezzy for you!'

Corrie heard them chasing each other about the sun-lounge as he went through into the kitchen, and then into the living-room, leaving the light off. He looked out through the front window towards the tree in the centre of the Green. No one was there yet.

There were bangs and slitherings from the back of the house, and Baskerville barked a couple of times. He sat in the dark for a short time, and then went back through into the sun-lounge. Baskerville was stretched out on the floor chewing an enormous bone.

'I got him so excited that he wet himself,' Jo said, wiping at the tiles with a mop. 'I've never had that effect on anyone before.'

Baskerville, grasping the bone on its end between his two front paws, shifted his position slightly, and the bone fell forward and hit him sharply on the nose. He looked startled, and scrabbled backwards.

'Baskervilles don't like bones.'

Jo put the mop and bucket back in the corner, and then walked towards Corrie. He had raised his eyebrows, and pulled the corners of his mouth down, in an expression of exaggerated innocence.

'I have my theories about you and Sal,' he said. 'The whole thing became clear to me when you sneaked away into the dining-room together, leaving me lying on the floor.'

'And I thought we were being so discreet.'

'It's obvious. She's studying you to use in her next novel. In the interests of research writers are sometimes compelled to undergo some very unpleasant experiences.'

'Do you think that my perversions . . .'

'Many and varied though they are . . .'

'. . . are advanced enough to interest her?'

Sal was quite well-known as a writer of novels for young people – 'New Adults' they were called by the publisher – usually dealing frankly with complex emotional or sexual difficulties.

'You could work on them a bit,' Jo said. 'Show a bit of imagination.' He looked at Baskerville. 'Why not have a passionate affair with Baskerville? I don't think she's used that one yet.'

Baskerville, looking vaguely troubled, edged away, and eyed Corrie with deep suspicion.

'He doesn't look too keen on the idea.'

'Poor old Baskerville. The dignified butt of vulgar jesting.'

Jo began to stroke Baskerville's head, and then continued speaking.

'She is good though, isn't she?' he asked. 'Her novels.'

'I enjoyed *Stephen's Child*.'

'*I Wish I Could Be Like David Jackson* was better. I don't know why people are so rude about them.'

'When they're not busy banning them from the children's departments in libraries.'

'That twit on television!' Jo began to speak in an excruciatingly cultured accent, one essaying a tone of heavy irony. ' "Sal Haggerty has left such trivia as pregnant schoolgirls behind long ago, and was one of the first in this country to break the menstruation and masturbation barrier. She has a very good line in masturbation." '

'Whatever that may be.'

'Whatever that may be.'

Corrie looked at his watch.

'The carol service will be starting soon.'

Jo searched for his wellington boots under the table.

'I expect we'll be the only people there. When they tell you that you're singing a solo, you do tend to imagine that you're not completely solo, and that there will be people there to listen to you.'

'You're the vicar in the empty church.'

'Verily.'

Jo stood up, and put the wellington boots on.

'I'm going to sing whether anyone's there or not.'

He looked at the wooden weather-house on the dresser. Both figures, the man and the woman, were inside the house, their backs turned on the outside world.

'I know just how you feel,' he said.

The telephone began to ring in the hall.

'I bet I know what that's about,' Jo said, and went out.

He came back in a few minutes later, nodding his head.

'Cancelled?'

'Cancelled. I'll just go and tell Lilli.'

When he came back in, Jo pulled on his anorak, and took down Pieter's umbrella.

'I said I was going to sing whether anyone was there or not.'

Corrie made a move towards the hall-way, to go out on to the Green from the front door, but Jo went out into the sun-lounge, and opened the door into the garden at the back of the house.

45

'Come on,' he said to Corrie. 'Quick, before Baskerville makes a break for it.'

Corrie had to bend down, sharing the umbrella with Jo, bumping into him, standing on his heels, until he took it from him, and held it over both of them. Jo led him out on to the path which ran alongside the end of the garden, along the top of the low cliff above the beach. He turned left, towards Gun Hill, and, some time later, wet and breathless, they were walking into St Edmund's churchyard.

He followed Jo, to stand in front of Mum's grave.

Jo took a torch out of his anorak pocket, and they looked at the writing on the gravestone.

There was a bunch of copper-coloured chrysanthemums on the grave, their petals separated and scattered about.

'They didn't last long in the rain,' Jo said.

Then, just as he had done in Lilli's dining-room, he began to sing, his head back, his hands thrust into his anorak pockets, his voice perfectly distinct above the sound of the rain on the umbrella, and on the ground around them, quite naturally and unselfconsciously.

> 'In the bleak mid-winter
>   Frosty wind made moan;
> Earth stood hard as iron,
>   Water like a stone;
> Snow had fallen, snow on snow,
>   Snow on snow,
> In the bleak mid-winter,
>   Long ago . . .'

As Jo sang, Corrie felt again the mood he had felt when he had looked at *The Wind in the Willows* calendar in the kitchen, and when he heard the words of the nativity at Lilli's: the sense of time passing, of things slipping away. It was the dying fall of the words 'Long ago'.

When Jo had sung at Lilli's Corrie had thought of Mum's funeral service. He had sat with his whole attention concentrated on the daffodils in the vase on the table at the front of the church, shutting out everything else around him, thinking of Rousseau, falling waters, unpopulated greenness.

He was known to be a polite boy, respectful, well-mannered, shy, but no one had seeemed surprised when he had broken out in the way he had, though it was so unlike him. He was taking his mother's death hard, was what they said. He would get over it in time. He had not been a very nice person, but they still seemed to think he was, even after the drugs episode, and the other things. How easily people can be fooled, he had thought, not with pleasure, aware of depths within himself he had yet to reveal, those little doors deep inside his head, doors that should never be opened.

Things were better now with Pieter, though he felt with Sal, as he felt with all his father's friends, that he had been discussed and analysed with her. Notes had been compared. Books and articles dealing with the strange science of parents and children had been suggested or loaned. Pieter would have been reassured that the difficulties he had been going through were common these days, in times like these. He would have come across them often enough, as a headmaster. Other children, too, had had problems. It was just a phase.

Over coffee, in any one of a dozen houses in Southwold, he would have been a subject of interest and concern. Women he hardly knew, who passed him in the street, and said, 'Hello, Corrie,' or 'How's your grandmother?' would be looking him up and down, and thinking of what they knew about him as they smiled and passed a few polite words. He would be sized up, the facts compared with the theories. *How did he seem to you?* They would know everything about him, the things he had said and done.

He felt the weight of other people all around him. Every time he left the house he had to prepare himself. A walk across the Green involved a need to greet and smile at half-a-dozen people. Because he was small and serious, adults often took it upon themselves to coax a smile out of him when he was alone with them. He dreaded being alone with Mr Arundel. He sometimes longed for a shop where he could go in and not be known, just buy a magazine or a packet of sweets, as he could in that shop in Lowestoft, without the need for the smile, the greeting, a few polite inquiries, the need to be good-natured, nice, a well-brought-up boy. They would report back in an interested, casual way, a subject for conversation, well-meant, wanting to help, but they would report back. *Cornelius was here this morning. How is he now?*

They nearly all seemed to be taller than he was. He was always the youngest in his class. He had started school a year early. He would be sixteen in a few days' time, just after Christmas, but he was still only 5 feet $3\frac{1}{2}$ inches tall. He seemed to have stuck at the same height for three years, and some of the clothes he had when he was twelve still fitted him. He had tried them on.

When Jo had finished singing, they moved out towards Church Street, to make their way back home.

Faintly, the voices had come out of the darkness and across the emptiness, high and clear in the cold air, shrill little voices singing of hope and steadfastness. The fir-tree is a symbol of faith. It is always green, in summer, and in winter, also, when it is snowing. It is noble and alone. It comforts and strengthens us.

Five

His copy of *Grimm's Fairy Tales* was an awkwardly large volume to read in bed. He had tried to read it lying on his side, but he had had to use both hands to hold the book, it was so heavy, and his wrists had ached painfully, and given way. He had ended by sitting up in bed, the book opened against his upraised knees beneath the bedclothes, his music notebook lying on top of his school atlas on the bed beside him.

He looked at Lilli's illustration for *Hansel and Gretel* on the wall at the side of his bed, studying it as he often did, lying in bed before he went to sleep.

> *Dr Ernst Jacoby*
> *Berlin-Charlottenburg*

24th November 1938.

Dear Sir,

Please allow us to tell you about our position, and about our hopes. We hope you listen kindly to the situation in which we and our family find ourselves. Mrs Katherina Viehmann has told us about your school, and about your kindness, and we have looked at your prospectus with great interest. We are friends of Mrs Viehmann.

You know, dear sir, how matters stand with us in Germany, and since the events of this month the situation for Jews in this country is developing and becoming worse.

49

We were compelled to give up our practices as doctors here, and, though it is now difficult to leave Germany without having a very particular reason for doing so, we hope to get government permission to emigrate to the United States. We need somewhere where our children will be able to continue their education and wait in safety while we try to carry out our plans. We ourselves make all efforts for leaving Germany, so that, within sight, the children could return in their father's house. It would also be good for them, for their English and for their health in the summer, because there are forbidden all the swimming-baths and all the parks.

We think our plans may take about a year to work. We do not know how long we will have to wait before we can leave the country, and, when we go to the United States, we do not think we could take the children with us, as it will be difficult for us at first to settle there and begin again.

We have three children: a girl of thirteen, a boy of twelve, and a boy of ten. They do not know any word of English, and if they learn well for a year, it will help them to settle in a school in America.

We have many questions to ask, which we hope do not trouble you.

Is it possible that you manage with our children, who do not know English? They know much, much less than Kurt and Thomas Viehmann when they first came to your school. Will it be too difficult for them with strangers in a foreign place? Is there, perhaps, a teacher who can speak German, so that, when, in the first time, they may feel unhappy, they would have someone who could listen to them? My wife and I speak English quite well, and we shall instruct our children so that they will have a little basis, and not feel so lonely if they can talk to their comrades. We will show them pictures so that England can become a place they can imagine. The oldest boy and girl have learned French and Latin in their 'Gymnasium'.

We do not know, perhaps this will help to learn English for them.

We are worried about the holidays, as the children will have no home. The children, as Jews, can only have passports which prevent them coming back to Germany again. Where could they go? Could they stay in the school? We know no one in England.

Your prospectus says the fee of 90L per annum. This part is difficult for us to write. We have a severe loss over the last five and a half years because of the situation here, and we are limited in our money. We will be allowed to leave Germany with a very little amount only, which we need to begin a new life in America. If you would be able to allow a special agreement for three children it would be valuable to us. We think we would be able to spend at the maximum 20L per month for all the three children. This payment will be safe when we are in America, because whatever new restrictions are made on the transfer of money from Germany this cannot be affected. Until this time, the children's grandmother in Warsaw, and a friend who is now living in Prague have agreed to pay, though it will be difficult for them. We do not think that we will be able to pay, ourselves, from Germany. We know the difficulties that Mrs Viehmann had.

Need we buy new clothes for them, the uniform and the equipment, if they will be only in England for a year? What should they bring in the way of suits and other necessities? Do the boys generally wear long trousers? What do they require for sport? Must they buy the required English school books already over here, or are they supplied in the school? Would they be allowed to wear ordinary clothes? It would be difficult for us to spend the money on many new clothes. Their clothes are not fashion clothes, but are suitable for children, and practical for school. Please excuse all these questions, but once the children are in England, they will have no money to buy anything.

51

If all works well, we hope our children can be at your school for the January term. When does the term begin? Could they stay somewhere before the term begins?

We hope you will listen to our questions with sympathy.

We ask you to tell us quite frankly whether you have any reason why you would prefer us not to send our children over. After recent events, you might see things from a different point of view, and we are anxious not to cause you or your school any difficulties. The position in Germany is such that we cannot make any firm promise to you about what might or what might not happen in the future, and the chances are that things will not turn better.

Our children are good and decent little people, and behave very well. You will not regret taking them into your school. Please don't mind the trouble we cause you. We love our country, but we must leave Germany.

> Yours sincerely,
> Dr Ernst Jacoby and
> Dr Madeleine Jacoby.

He opened *Grimm's Fairy Tales* again at *Hansel and Gretel*, and then turned the pages back to *The Wolf and the Seven Little Kids*, thinking of earlier that evening, when he was sitting on the step beside Jo, listening to Lilli reading. He had a reproduction of a Bewick woodcut as a bookplate in the book. Four little boys sat astride engraved and listing gravestones, riding them as though they were horses. They were dressed as soldiers.

He had just started re-reading the story, when he heard Jo moving about in his room next door. As he listened, he heard the school clock strike a single note, half-past eleven, its deep note followed by the higher single chime of the Dutch restaurant clock. The music did not play on the half-hour. Jo and he were the only people in Tennyson's: Matthias was sleeping in Lilli's house.

There was a louder bang from the next room, a sound like the bed being shifted.

He wondered if Jo had had another nightmare, and then if he were suffering from asthma again. He had looked a little hunched up earlier in the evening – the whole upper part of his body shrivelled in upon itself – and had gone to bed early, as soon as they had had Pieter's phone-call, about half an hour after they had arrived back from the churchyard. He occasionally experienced severe asthmatic attacks.

He pulled his dressing-gown on, and walked through into Jo's room.

The bedside light had been switched on, and Jo was standing beside his bed, pulling at the bedclothes.

'Hello, little Cornelius.'

'Hello, miniscule Johann.'

'You got me all excited then. I thought Santa was coming back for a second visit.'

'Have you done it again?'

Jo pulled a wry face, and nodded, indicating the wet sheets he was removing from the bed.

'Santa Claus had better wear wellies if he does call again.' He began to sing *I'm dreaming of a damp Christmas*. At irregular intervals, he had started to wet his bed, and there was a settled routine to be gone through when it happened.

'You get rid of the wet sheets, Jo. I'll remake the bed for you.'

'Perhaps I should have been trained with one of those musical potties,' Jo said. 'The ones that play a tune when you've produced something.'

'I always thought they were a rather sinister idea.'

'*Brave New Po.*'

'And I should think a lot would depend on the tune they chose.'

'What if they chose the National Anthem?'

'It could have disastrous consequences in later life. Just imagine, every time you heard that tune you'd . . .'

'. . . burst with patriotic fervour.'

53

'It could ruin a promising career in the Diplomatic Corps.'

'It could ruin several dozen pairs of socks.'

'And the dangers of a short-circuit . . .'

'It doesn't bear thinking about.'

The replies came rapidly, automatically. Jo could go onto automatic pilot, and carry on a conversation for a long time, with his mind absorbed completely elsewhere.

He had already washed himself and put on a dry pair of underpants. He slept in a T-shirt and underpants, the pants being easier to clean if he wet himself. He had a wide range of T-shirts with illustrations and slogans. The one he was wearing at the moment had *This Space to Let* printed across its front. He stood across the bed from Corrie as they bundled together the sheets and the waterproof cover. He always held himself very upright, like a small child being reprimanded, just as Corrie did.

'I thought you were putting up some Christmas decorations in here.'

'I decided it was not in the nature of boys to do that kind of thing.'

Jo walked out and went towards the bathroom, as Corrie took the spare sheets from the shelf in the cupboard, left ready by Lilli. There was the sound of a tap being turned on.

Jo came back in as Corrie was smoothing out the bottom sheet on the mattress. He stood and looked at him for a moment. He smoothed the bottom sheet carefully until it was absolutely free of wrinkles. Jo replaced the pillow on the bed, and took the other side of the top sheet.

'Can you think of any uses for a blanket?' Corrie asked, as they began to tuck one into the sides of the bed.

Richard Passenger had asked Jo's class once to spend an English lesson in writing down as many different uses as they could think of for a barrel, a paper-clip, a brick, and a blanket. Jo had thought of 117 uses before time had run out. Corrie had seen his list later. *A barrel can be used to float over the Niagara Falls. You have to be inside it, though. N.B. (1) You can get famous this way. N.B. (2) You can also get killed. A*

barrel can be used for making go-karts and things like that.
Boy scouts do this. Greggers is a boy scout, but I don't think
he makes go-karts out of things. You had better ask him. Better
still, I'll ask him, and the next time I do a piece of work for
you I'll put at the top whether he does or not. You can laugh
at a barrel. You can have a discussion group, and talk about
barrels. You can ignore a barrel. You can roll your trousers
up and climb inside a barrel, then roll down a hill, shouting
'Cheese!' or something like that. (It needn't be 'Cheese'. You
can shout whatever you feel like shouting.) The suggestion that
Corrie had liked best was that a brick could be a Bible for an
atheist.

Working together, in silence, they finished making the bed.

'Look at this,' Jo said, turning round and pulling down the
waistband of his underpants, as he climbed back into bed.
Age 7 was printed on the label in broad black lettering, beneath the manufacturer's name. 'Humiliating, isn't it?'

'It's no fun being a dwarf.'

'I found a poem about you the other day. *A Considerable
Speck*, it was called.'

'Oh yes. Robert Frost and I often went swinging on birches
together, until he fell off and killed his parrot.'

There was a long silence.

Jo sat up in bed, and arranged his sheets about him. He
looked like a child ill in bed in the middle of the day.

Corrie walked about the room, and sat down in the cane
rocking-chair, pushing himself backwards and forwards. Jo's
clothes were neatly folded on the trunk at the bottom of his
bed. The front of the thin sand-coloured jacket he had changed
into when they got back from the churchyard was covered in
metal badges. *I am 2. Head Girl. Netball Captain.* The badge
with Shakespeare's head, and *Will Power* on it was from when
they had gone to see the Royal Shakespeare Company in
London, during a short holiday the previous year.

The painting that Lilli had given to Jo, one of her illustrations for *The Six Swans*, hung above his bed. The rest of the
wall around the painting was covered by a large blown-up black

and white photographs of family and friends which Jo had taken and developed. The faces of himself, Pieter, Mum, Matthias, Lilli, Sal, Michael, Lincoln, Judith, Cato, and many others, regarded him from across the bed. He thought of Lilli's dining-room, and the intense close-up examination of the faces of the many people in all the paintings. The baby's face in the painting was at the very front of the painting, as it lay in its cradle beside its sleeping mother, and the evil Queen, her face hidden by a looped curtain at the other side of the room, was walking towards the baby, her hands just beginning to lift up from her side. There was a full-length photograph of himself directly opposite. He was wearing his high-heeled boots, that he wore to make him look taller, and jeans, and his hands were thrust into the slanting pockets of the hooded zip-front sweatshirt he was wearing. He was pulling a funny face.

He walked across the room.

'I pray you sit by us, and tell's a tale,' he said, sitting on the bed beside Jo.

'Merry or sad shall't be?'

'As merry as you will.'

'A sad tale's best for winter.'

He looked at Jo's T-shirt.

There was a fashionable shop in London selling T-shirts with the symbol of the Red Phoenix terrorists – the flame and the fist – on them. In the music magazine that Cato bought, next to an advertisement for teenage spots, he had seen an advertisement placed by a mail-order company for T-shirts with a line of bullet-holes printed across the front, to make it look as if the wearer had been machine-gunned. The shirts could also be ordered with bullet-holes printed on the back as well as the front, to look as if the bullets had gone right through the wearer's body. This cost fifty pence extra.

Jo looked ill, strained. There were dark lines under his eyes.

'O.K.?' Corrie asked.

Jo nodded.

'I thought your asthma had started when I heard you moving about.'

56

He told Jo about Matthias 'standing like Rupert the Bear', and they sat in silence for a while.

'Any more news about that school?'

Corrie shook his head.

'No. They just said again that they wanted the other terrorists releasing from prison before they'll set anyone free.'

'And the government won't let anyone be released?'

Corrie nodded.

'Just the same.'

'Just the same.'

'They can't do as the terrorists want, can they?' Jo asked. 'Release the prisoners? Because if they do, it'll happen again.'

'It will anyway.'

'How do you stop it happening in the first place?'

'You can't, can you?'

'The German government isn't going to negotiate, whatever happens.'

'Do you think they'll storm the building?'

'It's the only thing they can do.'

'The terrorists say they've got the children spaced out in different rooms. Imagine it in school here. Even if they got to one group in time, the other terrorists will have time to kill the children with them. They've got four whole classes. Nearly a half of the school. Could the army attack all the different rooms simultaneously?'

'Something's going to happen before long. Everyone seems to be co-operating. The Russians and East Germans haven't made any objections about all the troops being there. They've offered to help.'

'They've already killed five people. They've just been holding on to all those children for all this time.'

Jo flicked at the mobile hanging above his bed, a quick, angry action.

'They found somewhere to fly to when they'd killed Mum.'

Something cold brushed against Corrie's lips. It was one of the figures from the mobile. The eight silvery-metallic seagulls

57

swooped and soared in the slightest current of air. He moved back, rubbing at his mouth.

Their newspaper, *The Guardian*, had said *17 Killed in Airport Attack*. A more popular tabloid had had the headline *Good Friday Massacre*, adding *One Briton Believed Dead*. That had been Mum. She had been returning from a conference in Rome, a discussion of recent research into cancer. There was still hope of a breakthrough in finding a cure. She had gone even though she was pregnant. He had stared at the photographs in *The Guardian*: a man swabbing at a floor with a mop, two men carrying something in a blanket between them. When he was watching the news-report of the shooting at the school that afternoon he had leaned forward to see the body of the woman in more detail. He had wanted to see her face.

The usual clutter of extraordinarily assorted books lay on the carpet beside Jo's bed, around Corrie's feet: *The Little Prince*, *Kobbé's Complete Opera Book*, an American photographic magazine, *The Mouse and His Child*, a paperback edition of *Small is Beautiful* ('There's a book here about us,' he had said to Corrie when he had first bought it), an old school edition of *Emil and the Detectives*. His changes of subject-matter from day to day were unpredictable.

He had covered the front of his school rough-work book, lying clipped to his drawing-board, with his tiny neat printing. *Open only in case of earthquakes, tornadoes (gale force, assorted debris zooming about), custard pouring from volcanoes. Martians turning into cheese (Camembert), giant bats chewing gum in discotheques, the bus population going green (with ivy, not envy), celebration of annual haircut of Cato Levi, Saturnalia getting divorced from Copernicus, undulations in oscillating rhythm on British Rail track (1st class only) . . .* A length of wood, club-shaped, lay alongside the drawing-board, next to his flute, with the same style of printing on it in black felt-tip pen at the thinner end. *YOB BASHER. HOLD THIS END. Groin: 10 points. Legs: 3 points. Head: 25 points. Arse: 4 points.* At one end of it a black circle had been labelled *Self-destruction button.*

Corrie looked at it, and then picked it up.

He waved it at Jo, and spoke in a very refined and sophisticated voice.

'I say, how frightfully childish!'

'Well, we are children,' Jo said, quoting from *Emil and the Detectives*. He reached over the other side of the bed, away from Corrie, and pulled up his Winnie the Pooh, clutching it to him, and sucking his thumb noisily. In one sudden movement, he slid beneath the bedclothes, until only his eyes were visible above the sheets.

The ceiling had been entirely covered with Charlie Brown strip cartoons, clipped from a Sunday newspaper colour-magazine, bright primary colours of red, blue, and yellow. Corrie thought of the reproduction of Breughel's *Children's Games* hanging in the school San. He had seen it when he had gone to see Michael. Mechanically, joylessly, like troops drilled in some repetitive movement, the swarming children filling the streets played their games, each compelled to play the part of a child. Not a single child was laughing, or even smiling. With intense seriousness and concentration, they enacted all the actions expected of children, over and over again like clockwork figures in a wound-up toy. Unseen, in the distance, was a refuge, a place to which they could escape if they realised it was there, and could get away. Beyond the trees, beyond the river, open green fields stretched emptily away towards a wide horizon.

Beside Jo's bed was the light Corrie had thought of when he had seen the cake at Lilli's: a pottery model of the gingerbread house, made so that the light would shine through the windows of the house when it was switched on. The front was open, and miniature furniture inside was clearly visible: the table, the chairs, the tiled oven.

'Neely?'

'Yes, Jo-Jo?'

They were nicknames from early childhood, now used rarely, and half-jokingly.

'Tell me about Rousseau.'

This had been the usual request when he had sat on Jo's bed when he was younger.

Rousseau was the name of the mythical land Corrie had invented with Jo three years ago. Pieter had been working on the notes for his paperback edition of *Émile* when they had been trying to think of a name for their land. On the wall beside Jo's bed, alongside one of Lilli's posters for *The Winter's Tale*, was the large detailed map of Rousseau drawn in coloured inks by Jo. Other posters were on the other side of it: a photograph of the earth from space, a Peaceable Kingdom, the animals grouped around a standing lion, and the programme for the Victorian Evening. Corrie read the first lines.

Mama, Papa, Edmund, and young Albert
invite you to attend
A GLITTERING SOIRÉE.
Poetry, prose, music, and drama of an unimpeachable moral
tone, expressly for your delectation and edification.
Musicians:
Cello: Master C. Meeuwissen. Flute: Master J. Meeuwissen.
Violins: Mr and Mrs P. Meeuwissen.

Jo blew at the mobile, and the silver birds rose and fell, spinning above the bed.

'Wings soar in the silence.'

'Birds float above the sea.'

'Falling waters from the cliff-tops.'

'Lonely Rousseau waits for me.'

Jo grinned.

'You remember exactly.'

'I still go there sometimes.'

He could still write fluently and rapidly in the script and language they had invented for it. On the edges of the world, hidden by mist, lapped by the waters of an undiscovered sea, was the uninhabited solitude of that green and distant island. The only sound was that of the waterfalls, plunging down over rocks to the distant unprinted shore, and the sound of the music

60

that was inside his own head. It had become a real place to him, existing outside his own imagination, when he had looked at one of the art books at Lilli's, the Christmas they had stayed with her, and saw reproductions of paintings that were scenes from inside his own head – green leaf-fringed shadows in the depths of cool woods – and found that the painter's name was Rousseau.

'Wings soar in the silence.'

They both watched the silver birds slowly steady themselves, and stop.

'Do you think Matty liked his present?' Jo asked.

'Yes. He made enough noise with it.'

'It's just as well we had a German Christmas, and opened all our presents on Christmas Eve. Someone had told him about Father Christmas at play-school, and he was a bit scared of it happening in the middle of the night.'

'I don't blame him. How would you like a hairy old geezer coming into your bedroom when you're fast asleep?'

'Treading reindeer muck into your carpet. Anyway, if he goes off his present, I'll play with it instead.''

Jo emerged from beneath the bedclothes, and sat up beside Corrie.

He looked at him, thinking about something.

'Corrie . . . ?'

'Mmm?'

Jo hesitated for a moment, looked at Corrie again, and then reached down, and under his bed, bringing up a flat, square parcel in a plastic bag from a record shop. He placed it carefully on his knees, and smoothed his hands across the top of the bag, smoothing out all the wrinkles.

He spoke with his head down, looking down at his hands moving across the thin plastic.

'This is Mum's Christmas present.'

Corrie looked at him.

'I bought it last January, when we were in London in the New Year. It was just the right thing, and I had to buy it then. The records she had had got scratched. I kept it hidden in the bottom of the wardrobe.'

He looked up at Corrie, staring at him very closely.

'She's bound to have seen it, isn't she?'

'What did you get her?'

'The *Saint Matthew Passion*.'

Jo dropped his gaze, and looked down at the package on his knees again.

'You couldn't afford that, could you, Jo? That's four records.'

'They were having a sale. In Oxford Street. That's why I had to get it then. They'd had an incendiary bomb, and the box and the booklet had been damaged. They were selling a lot of records and things off cheaply. You know what it was like in London then.'

In the railway-stations, and on the underground, were warnings not to touch unattended packages or bags, and to report them to staff. They had had their bags searched several times, in theatres and concert-halls, museums and art-galleries. When they had gone to see the Royal Shakespeare Company, a man sitting in front of Corrie had left during the performance, and he had seen that the man had left a parcel under his seat. He had said nothing to anyone, afraid of making a scene, causing a disturbance, and had sat throughout the second half of the play – as Juliet sobbed, drank the drug, was lamented, as Romeo rode to Verona to join his bride in death, wept beside her body in a feasting presence full of light, as both Romeo and Juliet killed themselves, as the Montagues and Capulets were reconciled with tears over the bodies of their children – thinking only of the green Marks and Spencer carrier-bag lying on its side in front of him. Beneath the surface of everyday life, nothing was what it seemed, and mutilation could lie beneath the commonplaces of the day-to-day: a car, a pillar-box, an unattended parcel, an envelope with unfamiliar hand-writing. In nearby streets were the sounds of the sirens.

Jo slid the contents out of the plastic bag. He had made a new box to hold the four records, and, in watercolours, had

62

painted a cover showing the road to Calvary. He had done it beautifully, copying the style of one of Lilli's paintings.

He had painted the interior of a family house, rooms opening out into deeper rooms through open doors, each room represented in close detail. In the different rooms, glimpses of a family could be seen, dressed in the fashion of the 1930s: a woman sewing, a boy bent over a toy, a man peering through his spectacles at a book, a little girl stroking a cat. Through one of the windows, unseen by any of the family, a casual detail almost lost in the general pattern of the picture, a crowd in the street were watching someone who had fallen down. His feet were just visible at the edge of the window. A man was standing fully visible, just above the fallen figure, his arm about to rise and bring a whip down upon him. The faces of the crowd were not gleeful or excited. They were just gazing blankly at the occurrence of events over which they had no control. One or two were smiling. A few were averting their eyes.

Jo ran his hand around the edge of the box.

It had been their mother's favourite of all Bach's works. It had been played at her funeral.

'She's bound to have seen it, isn't she? Isn't she, Corrie?'

The school clock began to strike midnight. They both listened until it had finished, and the echoes had died away. The bells of the clock above the Dutch restaurant chimed, and then began to play their folk-song.

'Happy Birthday, Jesus.'

'Happy Christmas, Jo.'

'*Fröhliche Weihnachten*, Corrie. I enjoyed Lilli's German Christmas.'

63

Six

'Beside a dark pathless forest there lived a poor woodcutter with his second wife and his two children, a little boy and a little girl. The boy was called Hansel and the girl Gretel. They had very little to eat, and when a great famine came to the country, the father found it impossible to find them any food at all. One night when the children were in bed, he lay thinking of what he could do for them all. Overcome with fear, he groaned, and said to his wife, "What can we do? How can we feed our poor children, when we can't even feed ourselves?"

' "I know exactly what we can do, husband," answered the stepmother. "Tomorrow morning, very early, we will take the children into the midst of the forest, where it is darkest, light a fire for them, give them each one last piece of bread, and then we will go off to work, and leave them there, and never return. They will not be able to find their way home again, and we shall be free of them."

' "No, my wife," said the father, horrified, "we cannot do that. I could not bear to leave my poor children alone in the forest. The wild animals will tear them to pieces."

' "Fool!" said the woman. "If we do not do this, then all four of us will die of hunger. We must destroy them in order to live ourselves. Otherwise you might as well start making the coffins for us all now."

'The man's heart grew heavy, and he would not agree with

64

her. She did not leave him alone until he had agreed to her plan. He said to himself, "It is not right," and yet he agreed.

' "I still feel very sorry for my poor children, whatever you say," said the father.'

He sat on the window-seat in the first floor bedroom at the back of The Ferry House, holding the postcards from Katherina Viehmann, and Peter and Aline Goetzel. The door set into the wall was open, and piles of carefully-stacked papers were on the floor at his feet. He was leaning over, reading *Hansel and Gretel* from the *Grimm's Fairy Tales*, lying open on the window-seat beside him, next to his music notebook, on top of his atlas. It was the afternoon of 28th December, his birthday.

He had always written music, increasingly so over the past two years, short pieces to be performed by The Elizabethan World Picture, or by his family, and he had written songs for Levi's, a group formed by Cato Levi, his friend at school. (Cato had kept reminding him that his grandfather had been Michael Meeuwissen, whose *Folk Songs of Europe* was still in print.) After the success of his music for *The Winter's Tale*, Richard Passenger, the teacher who had produced the play, asked him, during the party after the last night, if he had ever thought of writing the music for an original opera or musical to be performed in school.

That was all he had said, but it had stayed in Corrie's mind.

Just after the end of term, he had been lying in bed one night, his eyes upon the *Hansel and Gretel* painting.

There was something he felt a need to express about those two figures.

Hansel and Gretel moved and affected him deeply – it was a story he had read and re-read as a small child, and in the last few months – and he felt that he wanted to convey what he felt the story was trying to say, the atmosphere of Lilli's painting. It had been a mood, rather than a clear conception of what he might do, like the struggle for words in trying to give a vivid description of a half-forgotten dream, but it had come to him that he might be able to express his feelings through music. Over the past week he had started to sketch out ideas for a musical adaptation of the story. He wanted to make it free of the kind of inaccuracies he had seen in previous adaptations. Unlike the Humperdinck opera, there would be no caring parents, no Sandman, no Dew Fairy, no guardian angels.

Berlin-Charlottenburg.

14.X.1935.

Dear Mr High,

Please send me a prospectus of your school. I write having received the best recommendation of Your school by Mrs Viehmann, my dear friend, who I know since years. I must send my two children from Germany, a boy of twelve, and a girl of ten. As German Jew I have to select the Institut not only for the study, but I am forced to seek a school, the fees of which are corresponding to my reduced capital. I am a woman author, and my husband is a lawyer. We are both since 2 years without possibility of earn money. I hope You understand my incorrect English.

Yours faithfully,

Ruth Grünbaum.

When he had opened the door set into the bedroom wall of The Ferry House, his ideas had started to form more clearly. The mood had crystallised, given form by what he had seen, and the structure had begun to emerge: a cantata, with a narrator, a chorus, and mime, rather than a conventional operatic or musical treatment. *Auf meines Kindes Tod* was to be the final song for the chorus.

He picked up his bookmark in *Grimm's Fairy Tales*, and looked again at Nickolaus Mittler's postcard.

Please pardon me about my stammerings, but my will is

66

stronger than the words I know. We will be diligent in our study and becomingness, and prove ourselves worthy. We will be good boys.

The main frontage of Southwold School filled the south side of Dunwich Green, the southernmost of all the Greens in Southwold, but the music rooms were some distance behind the rest of the school buildings, in The Ferry House, an early Victorian building. It had been the original headmaster's house until Tennyson's, on the east side of the Green, backing on to the low cliff above the beach, had been built in the time of the third headmaster. Tennyson's was one of a terrace of Edwardian houses, each with a different white head above its arched doorway, gazing out across the Green. Passers-by who walked along the western boundary of the school fields, down the footpath which led from the town towards the ferry across the River Blyth, often heard confused fragments of music as they passed The Ferry House in term-time.

His favourite room for practice was a first-floor room at the back of the building, looking out across the school playing-fields towards the sea, beyond the wall and the low sand-dunes. It had originally been one of the bedrooms in the house, high-ceilinged, tall-windowed, beautifully-proportioned, with an ornate white-painted fireplace curly with leaves and bunches of grapes. He would borrow the key from his father – it helped, sometimes, to be the headmaster's son – and spend hours there in the long holidays, when all the boarders had gone home, and there was no one there to disturb him, bent over his cello, at the piano, or just sitting in the cold bare room, above the quiet, wall-enclosed fields.

On the morning of Christmas Eve, sitting on the window-seat of the practice-room, he had looked down at Jo, acting as a goalkeeper for Matthias on the First Eleven football pitch. Immediately after breakfast he and Jo had spent an hour or so together in The Ferry House, practising *Auf meines Kindes Tod*, and the other musical pieces they were going to perform for the German Christmas. Jo kept making spectacular and carefully unsuccessful attempts to save the goals that Matthias kicked in from six feet away. Matthias, knees bent, had to pump his arms up and down to keep his balance, and occasionally fell flat on his face. He was encrusted in mud, and the fine drizzle of the early morning was intensifying into rain. Baskerville hung uncertainly about in the background, occasionally making hesitant little forays towards them.

Usually, his father had given him the single key to open the door of The Ferry House when he had wanted to go there to practice in the holidays. As his father was away, Corrie had taken the complete bunch of Ferry House keys from the office, without bothering to remove the one key he usually used.

He had sat down on the window-seat, jingling the bunch of keys in his hand, spinning them round on the ring. He had been practising his cello for two hours.

Set in the wall of the bedroom was a locked door, and he had often wondered what was behind that door. It was a panelled white-painted door with a brass handle.

On the key-ring was a little key he had not seen before.

He had moved away from the window, and up to the inset door.

He thought he would just walk past it, but he began to wonder what was behind that door. It was a door like any other door. He examined the little key carefully. It was a key like any other key. He put the key in the keyhole, turned it only a little, and the door was open.

Beyond the bedroom door he had stepped into darkness.

He had stood for a moment until his eyes had become accustomed to the dim light. It was a long, narrow, windowless room, like a boarded-over railway-carriage. Slatted wooden shelves stretched away against the walls on both sides, stacked with dusty files of old incoming school mail.

The floor was white with the spilled contents of files which had fallen.

68

He had squatted down in the dusty darkness, disappointed, mildly interested, and picked up the letters lying nearest to him on the bare boards, letters from the late 1930s, letters about the trivial important concerns of childhood: a boy to have milk in his cocoa, a boy not to have eggs, discovered smokers, requests for details of entrance to the school, a new school heating-system, an accident to a boy in a games-lesson, the payment of fees.

Then, idly sifting through the papers at his feet, like the valueless litter left in an abandoned room, he had come across the first of the letters which had made him pause, and then move across to read them sitting down, on the window-seat above the playing-fields, his brothers' voices sharp in the air around him. Doors had begun to open, deep inside his head.

Ministry of Labour.
July 1939.

Military Training Act, 1939.

I am directed by the Minister of Labour, in pursuance of the powers conferred upon him by Section 10 of the Military Training Act, to request that you will be good enough to furnish a return of information required by him with respect to certain persons who have attended your school.

Persons of whom information is required. The return should relate to all boys born between the 4th June, 1918, and the 3rd June, 1919, both days included, who have been on the school roll in your school at any time during the last five years.

Information to be included in the return. The particulars desired to be furnished in respect of each boy are: full name, date of birth, home address and name of parent or guardian.

Form of return. It is desired that the particulars should be furnished upon cards which will be supplied to you for the purpose. One card should be used for each individual.

69

A postcard form is enclosed upon which you are requested to notify to the Registrar General, Somerset House, London, W.C., the number of cards estimated to be required for the return. On receipt of the postcard, the requisite supply of cards will be forwarded to you.

I would add, after our earlier correspondence, that this return is asked for, not as an act of voluntary co-operation, but as a statutory duty imposed by Section 10 of the Military Training Act. A refusal to comply with the Minister's request would thus constitute a breach of the provisions of the law.

Civilian Protection Ltd.
Warwick Plain, Coventry.

8th June 1939.

Dear Sir,

We are pleased to be able to offer the supply of the following for the use and protection of the pupils under your control.

(i) IDENTIFICATION DISCS. The sensible suggestion has been made that the civilian population should have some readily available means of identification about them. We believe that, for children, the best possible method is the wearing of one of our clearly printed METAL IDENTIFICATION DISCS. Each disc can bear the name of the pupil and the school, and will be a great advantage to you in identifying a pupil quickly in case of any difficulties encountered as a result of an airraid.

(ii) STRETCHERS. Our models are constructed of metal and fold easily for storage. There is no canvas to become discoloured or rot, and they may readily be hosed down if they become contaminated.

Our prices are most reasonable. The stretchers, for example, cost only 48/- each, but there is a considerable reduction if you place an order for more than a dozen.

We respectfully await your instructions.

Yours faithfully,

J. L. Carter,
Sales Manager.

Emergency Committee for the Care of German
Jewish Children.

Rachel House,
London W.1.
11th July 1938.

Dear Anthony High,

You have done so much for our children, that I hesitate to burden you any further, but you will realise the desperate urgency of the situation in Germany. Perhaps the Evian Conference will be able to find a solution, but we have hundreds of people who just cannot wait longer. There has been an enormous rise in applications for help. I am sure that you yourself will have become aware of this from Leonie Matthias in Berlin.

Please forgive me if I ask you to please give me a brief indication of any further help you feel able to offer. Have you room for any children at all in September? Do you specify any particular ages? How many boys could you take? Could you take any more girls? What is the lowest possible figure you would be willing to accept as fees? (As you know, it is virtually impossible to get any money out of Germany.) Would you be willing to allow me to act on your behalf in accepting any children? I give you my assurance that the Committee and I will make the fullest investigation of each case.

We are keenly aware of the generosity of yourself and your Committee, and you may feel that you have done all you could be reasonably expected to do, but we hardly know where to turn, and we need to get as many children out of Germany as possible, and as quickly as possible.

Each place offered would mean that one more child was safe.

I would be very grateful if you could reply soon. With renewed thanks.

Yours sincerely,
Hannah Greif.

Below him, on the football pitch, Matthias and Baskerville had seemed to hit upon a co-ordinated plan, and Jo did a complete back-somersault over Baskerville, and nearly ended up with his head jammed beneath the net. 'You're supposed to be the referee!' he complained fiercely. 'Canine nutter!' Matthias began to dance about because he had scored, moved more quickly than his legs could keep up with, and fell over. The high clear voices floated up from the field, and he had felt the vague, powerful forces of the adult world beginning to gather, waiting, at the edges of childhood, unseen by the children. How low were the walls around the school, how near the world outside.

The next thing he had picked up had been the postcard from Nickolaus Mittler, posted on June 20th, 1939.

He had spent the rest of the morning in trying to sort his way through the massed and scattered papers on the floor in the inner room, beginning to arrange them in different piles, to approach some rough chronological order. On the afternoon of Christmas Day he had left the others watching *The Wizard of Oz* on television. Dorothy had just started to follow the yellow brick road. On each day since then he had come down to The Ferry House, saying that he was going to practise his cello. Patiently, carefully, he had tried to trace his way through the files of correspondence, beginning in 1933. The flimsy, yellow papers were like documents from centuries ago, unfamiliar moustached or bearded figures on faded stamps with tiny denominations.

He knew that the school had been evacuated during the war, and the staff and children moved away, when Southwold had been declared a prohibited area. The records for the 1930s and 1940s were disorganised and incomplete, probably as a result of this, and some of the 1930s files – whole stretches between 1934 and 1938 – seemed to have been lost or destroyed. There were three files for each year – heavy box-files with rusted metal clips inside – usually exactly divided into four-month periods, but some were unsorted, random piles of documents from different years bundled together, and damaged by fire, scorched or partially burned. In all the files, and strewn about the floor, in increasing numbers as the years went by, were the many letters from Jewish families in Germany, a part of the past of Lilli, and of himself.

It was difficult, with the incompleteness and confusion of the files from the dark inner room, to follow through the correspondence of individual families over the years – some names just seemed to vanish, and with others it was unclear whether or not children had actually managed to get to the school – but, as he approached the final file of late 1939, he had got to know some of the families well. Intent, absorbed, he read on, unable to draw himself away, as the letters and postcards poured in from Berlin, month after month, sometimes couched in the awkward English of commercial communications, asking if there was any possibility of a vacancy at the school: ordinary men and women, mothers and fathers, decent people, trying to learn how to plead, for themselves, and for their children.

He placed the two postcards on the window-seat in front of him, side by side.

Berlin-Charlottenburg 4.
15th May 1934.

Dear Sir,

I would be happy if you could please be so kind to send me a prospectus of your school. I was given your address by Miss Leonie Matthias, 'Elternhilfe für die jüdische Jugend'. My boys whom I want to send to England are 10 years old and 13 years old. They have some knowledge of English, and can understand when people speak English to them, but they cannot really speak. More than 60L each for a year I cannot devote to my boys' education. I know it is a small sum. We are Jews. Will this mean difficulties in the school with their comrades? We are not political, and do not belong to any organisation. We have a great desire to give our sons under your care.

Yours faithfully,
Frau Katherina Viehmann.

Berlin-Charlottenburg 2.
18th January 1938.

Dear Mr High,

I need an attestation for the german authorities that my daughter Charlotte Goetzel is going to Southwold School. Please send me this paper in the next days.

Lotte cannot speak English and it is the first time that she is separated from her home and from her parents. She is our only child. Please treat her with great love and solicitude. Please, if you have a little time, let us know whether you are content with her.

Thank you for your kind help in our bad circumstances.

With sincere good wishes,
Peter and Aline Goetzel.

He turned the two postcards over, and again studied the sepia photographs carefully.

Blick vom Hotel Adlon auf den Pariser Platz, im Hintergrund Tiergarten, Siegessäule, Reichstag, Berlin. (Sight from the Hotel Adlon on the Parisian Place. In the background the Tiergarten, column of victory, parliament-building, Berlin.)

The Brandenburg Gate, with its six banks of neo-classical columns, the triumphal arch at the start of Berlin's major central thoroughfare, seemed like a gate in Roman times, a clear boundary between the city and the countryside. In front of the Gate, the wide empty expanse of the start of Unter den Linden stretched away. On the right, buildings were crammed together, as though crowded within the walls of an overpopulated and rapidly-growing city, the square towers and shallow central dome of the Reichstag rising above everything else. Behind the Gate, as though it were wild and open countryside, were the trees of the Tiergarten. Beyond these was Charlottenburg, and all the other fashionable western suburbs, safe, middle-class, comfortable. From amongst the trees of the Tiergarten, Victory rose up on her column, and, above the Gate, another figure of Victory, in a chariot pulled by four horses, faced down Unter den Linden.

Reichstagsgebäude und Brandenburger Tor, Berlin. (Parlia-ment-building and Brandenburger Gate, Berlin.) To the left, and to the right, of a wide empty avenue were the Reich-stag and the Brandenburg Gate. Tram-lines curved round on the left, beyond an area of grass, and, beyond them, were the stone pillars lining the sides of what seemed to be the beginning of a bridge, stone urns on top of stone columns at either side of it. A double-decker bus had just crossed between the stone columns, and was in the middle of the broad deserted road. Leafless trees rose beyond the bus and beyond the bridge, and, behind these, the Reichstag stood. A squat tower was at either side of the massive main frontage, and, beyond these, rising above the centre of the whole square building, was a low dome surmounted by a pinnacle. Across the road, on the right, at the end of the buildings lining that side of the street, was the Brandenburg Gate, its columned frontage facing the entrance to the bridge. On top of this, the figure of Victory on her chariot, raised her arms heavenward, her back turned towards the whole scene, facing away from the columns, the colonnaded bridge, the dome, and the bus. The Gate appeared to be a solid structure with no way through.

On Christmas Day, in one of the surviving files for 1933, he had found the first letter from Rachel House, and then all the other letters, some of them on the floor around him.

*Emergency Committee for the Care of German
Jewish Children*

*Rachel House,
London W.1.*
19th July 1933.

Dear Mr High,

Do you remember me from fifteen years ago, when we both served on the Stewart-Hamill Committee? I remember you (and Mrs High) well, and how pleased you both were because David had just started to speak. (Yes, it was a long time ago!) I remember, also, how, as a result of the findings of this Committee, you were so ready to give free places to five of the starving Austrian children, and how you felt the happiness that resulted was as great for you as it was for them.

We are just one of many agencies and organisations endeavouring to help German refugees – pacifists, professional people, Jews, evangelicals etc. – but our particular concern, as our name indicates, is with German Jewish children. I realise that we are certainly not unique in this field, and I am afraid that the number of agencies so concerned will increase rapidly and inevitably if the current situation in Germany intensifies. I do hope that I can presume on a previous acquaintanceship to seek your help. Here at Rachel House we are trying to help refugee Jewish children whose parents are in concentration camps, or deprived of their means of livelihood. We have established close contact with a Jewish organisation in Berlin (Miss Leonie Matthias, 'Elternhilfe für die jüdische Jugend', Berlin-Charlottenburg, Tiergartenstrasse), and hope to work together to alleviate the suffering caused by the actions of the present German government.

Could you take two or three of these children in September? Even a tentative promise 'subject to the approval

76

of the School Committee' will be helpful. Are there other headteachers in your area who might also be willing to help, with boys or girls? Would you be able to offer places to girls at your school? (We hope to keep brothers and sisters together.) I will be happy to supply you with any further details, or answer any questions.

I hope that you will feel able to help.

Yours sincerely,
Hannah Greif.

Dr Wilhelm Viehmann
Berlin-Charlottenburg 4.
23rd September 1934.

Dear Mr High,

Thank you very much for your letter from last week. My husband found the week he spent in England when he brought our boys a very happy time. He has told me all about Southwold, and about meeting you and your family.

The start of life in England, and the beginning of term in a new school, have been very great events for our boys, and Kurt and Thomas write very much in their letters about it, and show a happiness they have not known for many months. Their letters talk much of their sport-life, and I am very glad that they are involved in this traditional 'fair sport' side of English manner of life.

Kurt is beginning to imitate the English orthography, and he does progress. He is beginning to write the nouns with the small letters in the correct way. He is telling me he is knowing the language 'jolly well'. Thomas, I think, is a little homesick. He is gentler in mind than Kurt, and more longing for tenderness. Everyone he knows in the world is in Germany. I hope that he will accustom more and more to your life and will be a good comrade among the other boys. Are you satisfied with their progress in English, and with their behaviour?

I hope my husband tried to tell you how thankful we

both are that our boys are in your school during this difficult time and learn all about English life, but he does not speak English well. *My* English is not enough to express to you all the thankfulness we feel towards you and your school. I could not express it in German. You hardly know what a relief it is for us in our situation that our children are taken care of in your community, where they can be children, without the troubles of the adult world. I am so grateful that, with comrades of their own age, they will perhaps forget soon what they were compelled for so many months to endure, with the sorrows of grown-up people, the many conflicts and pains they have suffered in their native country. With a heavy heart we sent them away, but we feel comforted knowing you care for them in our bad times. It is a marvellous experience in our life to find friends in a country where we are only strangers. People are kind. We must remember this.

With many thanks for all your kindness towards us and our children. Kindest regards, also, to Misses High, please. The boys' grandmother, also, sends her good wishes.

Yours thankfull,

Frau Katherina Viehmann.

Please give my love to my boys. I wait for their Sunday letters. I hope their colds are better.

London W.C.1.

22nd Oktober 1935.

Very respected Mr High,

I have heard of your school through my friend Kurt Viehmann who has been a pupil at your school since one year, who ask you that I please would be accepted also.

I am 14 years old, a German Jew, as Kurt is. I went in Berlin to the same 'Gymnasium' as Kurt, and you may ask there a report about me. I was good student. I have my school reports with me here in England, and can show them to you. My wish is to be a physician.

My parents' letter will arrive soon. They told me to ask

you if I could be allowed in your school. They have told me that if I can find a school to take me, I need not go back to Berlin. Please let me come to your school, Mr High. I beg to ask that you will accept me. My parents will not be able to afford that I come to England a second time. My fees will be paid monthly, which you will receive directly from my uncle in Paris, in French francs.

I am already one week in London, and my permission to remain in this country is soon expiring. I soon must return to Berlin if I find no school. You would oblige me very much if you let me know your decision soon.

Yours respectfully,

Rudolf Seidemann.

P.S. Please deliver my best regard to Kurt. Thank you.

Emergency Committee for the Care of German Jewish Children.

Rachel House,

London W.1.

7th February 1936.

Re Kurt and Thomas Viehmann.

Dear Anthony High,

I was in Berlin over the New Year, and I'm afraid that the extraordinarily stringent financial restrictions operated by the German authorities are going to lead to some heart-breaking situations. Thousands of German refugees are going to find it virtually impossible to get help, or to leave the country. Life is made unbearable for them, so that they are driven to make arrangements to leave the country, and then it is made so difficult for them that they are unable to carry out their plans.

I saw Kurt and Thomas's mother, and no one could be more full of gratitude than she is for you and Southwold, and what you are doing for her sons. Her only comfort in her current situation is to know that they, at least, are safe in England.

But we don't know what we can do about the school fees. When they sent their boys to England in 1934, they felt sure that they knew of a safe and permanent way to get money out of Germany to pay the boys' fees, but they now realise that they were mistaken. Things have tightened up fiercely. They have tried every possible way to transfer money to England, but, of course, they have no relations outside Germany who could help them.

They thought, at one stage, of your finding English people who were going to travel for holidays in Germany, and who would need German currency for their stay. You could have given these tourists their address in Berlin, and a slip with your signature, and they would have given the money for the fees to these people, who would repay you in English money when they returned home. Just before this happened, the boys could have written home to tell their parents that friends were going to visit them from England to give them the latest news from school, informing them of their names, to act as a safeguard. I felt that this was really too dangerous a plan.

Another idea they had considered recently was to support a child in need – chosen by a British charity in Berlin – and to arrange for an equivalent sum to be transferred via the charity to England to pay for the boys' school fees: but this would not have been permitted, as I had to point out. Their final idea – and they really are desperately anxious to fulfil their commitment – is to have English children staying as their guests in Berlin for some time, if the children's parents would agree, in exchange, to pay for the fees of Kurt and Thomas. I understand that when the boys returned home for the Christmas holidays, Kurt brought an English schoolfriend home with him, and they showed him all the sights of Berlin, and he had a very enjoyable time. Is there any possibility of this working?

If not, the Viehmanns will be quite unable to pay the boys' school-fees.

There are going to be many more similar cases, where

children do not have relations outside Germany willing to pay for them. What can we do? The clearing systems are totally inadequate for the huge volume of finance which should be passing through for school-fees. We have such limited resources, and so many cases on our books, that the Commitee have decided that we cannot possibly accept any new cases under any circumstances for the payment of fees through the Exchange Clearing. We, therefore, will be unable to offer any financial assistance for Kurt and Thomas Viehmann, and have told Mr and Mrs Viehmann of the failure of their plans.

You might feel that the only possible answer is that the boys must be sent back into Germany, as you can hardly justify their staying on at your school, but I know that you will be fully aware of the effect of this news on Kurt and Thomas. I know what it is like for Jewish children in Berlin schools. I am so very sorry.

Yours sincerely,
Hannah Greif.

Dr Wilhelm Viehmann
Berlin-Charlottenburg 4.

15th February 1936.

Dear Mr High,

I have heard the news from 'Elternhilfe für die jüdische Jugend' about the news from the 'Rachelhouse'. I do not want you to believe that our non-payment is deliberate. It is for us a matter of course and honour to pay the fees as soon as the German regulations will allow this. We do not know what to do. Yesterday I walked to see Mrs Kirchner, who I know wrote to you about her two children, and said she was aided by the Clearing-House of 'Elternhilfe' for paying her fees. I wished to discover how she had succeeded so well. But I was sad when her statements were vague, and found she was only pretending. Mrs Kirchner is only on the waiting-list, just as I am. I do not blame her for what she said. She had been told that her son Alex's turn had come (after eighteen months waiting) and then they announced to her that they were doing nothing for boys under fourteen.

I applied again to 'Elternhilfe' for news of my position on the waiting-list for the Clearing-House for the money, and hope to hear a clear answer by next week. I hope that then we shall be able to transfer a sum of money to pay the money we owe you soon. It is difficult for us now to travel to England, since we have lost our German citizenship.

We are very gratefull for all you have done for our boys. You have given them back their bright childhood, and made it possible for them to build up their lives. Please trust us, Mr High. We shall do all we can to pay the money. Please excuse the trouble we are obliged to arise. I ask if you will allow our boys to remain in your school. You understand I would not ask if I would not be obliged to do so. We have caused you so many worries and difficulties.

Thank you for all your help to Kurt and Thomas, and to us.

Affectionately yours,
Katherina Viehmann.

Aliens Department. Home Office, Whitehall.
4th April 1936.

With reference to your letter of the 26th March, I am directed by the Secretary of State to say that he regrets that he is not prepared to entertain an application for the grant of a certificate of naturalization to Kurt Erich Viehmann during his minority.

I am, sir,
Your obedient servant,
J. Dickson.

Berlin-Charlottenburg 2.
5th April 1938.

Dear Mr High,

Only today we got a letter from Lotte which rather afraid us. It is, we think, a little lonely for her by herself in the holidays. She seems to feel so lonely and homesick, and thinks she has no friends. She misses, also, her little dog. She seems to weep every night, and we worry about our dear daughter. She writes absolutely unhappy in the idea not to get through the examination! Lotte feels so anxious about the Mathematics. We hope that this is only a nervousness of hers. Were you satisfied with the results of her report-book? She tells us that the doctor told her she should swim and lead an active life, and not worry too much about herself.

Lotte tells us that no payment has reached you from my brother in Palestine. Please remember him if by mistake a payment should be late. I wrote to my brother with this sense, and he says it would only be on account of the difficulties in sending, but he is sure he will be able to manage it. If there are any questions of this kind, please, dear Mr High, do not tell the child about them. Lotte feels very upset.

The 15th April is Lotte's birthday. Would you kindly buy her a little chocolate? It is almost impossible for us to send it abroad. We want to help Lotte, but we feel so helpless.

Excuse, please, these problems.
Peter and Aline Goetzel.

Berlin-Charlottenburg.
15th June 1939.

Dear Sir,

Mrs Greif did write to Miss Matthias from England and tell me the acception of me and my big brother as pupils of your school next term at a fee of £55 p.a. which enable us to fulfil our one wish to continue with our learning and our music. My father will send you the Form and Application for Admission. I only wish to thank you for your extreem kindness.

Yours very grateful,
Nickolaus Mittler.

The photograph on the other side of Nickolaus Mittler's first postcard was of Berlin Cathedral. He had never known that Berlin had had a cathedral.

Dom mit Umgebung, Berlin. (Flugzeugaufnahme.) Cathedral and his environment, Berlin. (Sight·from the aeroplane.)

The immense Baroque dome reared up from the centre, bigger than all the rest of the building, a smaller dome at each of its corners. It reared up, much bigger than any of the buildings beyond it, across a river, a sculptured mass to dominate any city skyline. A bridge crossed the river behind it, to its left, dwarfed by the soaring dome. The aggressively ornate ecclesiastical architecture overpowered the severe classicism of the Alter Museum beside it, and it appeared top-heavy, about to topple backwards, and sink beneath the river, pulled down by the weight of that enormous dome. The view from the air had been taken by a plane swooping low across the building, like a bomber about to jettison its cargo, and destroy the whole immense edifice by explosion and fire, sending it toppling down into heaps of blackened rubble.

A cold wind was blowing down a broad street lined with balconied apartments. Most of the shutters were closed, and all the doors were locked.

He saw a lonely face at a window.

Inside a second-floor apartment, Nickolaus Mittler was slowly, patiently, writing at a table near the window, bent over, intent. Loose papers, postcards, books, and dictionaries were around him. The boy wrote and wrote, card after card, the pen-nib scratching in the silence of the room. Behind him, in the corner of the room, beside the window, her head turned towards it, a woman stood very still, as though listening for a

84

sound outside in the street. In the hall, packed suitcases were lined against the wall. The suitcases were expensive, but the hall was empty of furniture, and the walls were bare, A man, and an older boy, sat on the uncarpeted boards of the floor, beside the telephone. They were all wearing their best clothes.

Behind the four still, rapt figures, open doors led through to other doors, deeper inside, other rooms, other lives, just out of sight, closed doors opening deeper and deeper inside.

In opening that door into that hidden room, he had opened the door inside his own head that he had found at Lilli's two years ago, into one of the deeper rooms inside that darkness within himself, deeper rooms unlocking as he began to search his way towards the innermost room, the darkness of the events that began in Germany in the 1930s, towards the fir-trees, and the heart of that dark pathless forest.

Seven

During his early lessons with Lilli he had made use of his school atlas, giving her the names of places – Dresden, Berlin, Southwold, King's Lynn, London – she had to find and point out to him. On page 14 both parts of Germany were coloured the same pale orange colour, as though the country were whole, and it was the time before the war.

Lilli's finger poised in the air above the open atlas, moved down – *Spandau, Potsdam, Brandenburg, Charlottenburg* – and came firmly to rest upon Berlin.

Berlin, like Vienna to the south of it, was so enormous a city that it was not represented, even on the small-scale map of the school atlas, as a dot or a square, but as an irregular solid area of grey to show the extent of the built-up area. Charlottenburg, where the Viehmanns and Nickolaus Mittler lived, where so many of the Berlin letters and postcards came from, was a large western suburb of Berlin, a circle as large as any independent town at the edge of the vast, unknown city.

He had a picture in his mind of Germany in the early 1930s, before the bombs started falling, before all the millions of people were led away into the darkness, a picture made up from books he had read, films and television documentaries he had seen.

In the countryside lived girls called Heidi, with braided blonde hair, who stood on the mountainsides with their hands on their hips, smiling, in dazzlingly bright sunshine. They

86

wore white blouses with big puffed sleeves, little white embroidered aprons, and lace-up bodices like the one that the Walt Disney version of Snow White wore. Unlike Snow White, they had big breasts. Every mountainside was crowded with big-breasted blonde girls with their hands on their hips, simpering at the camera. All the men were called Fritz and wore leather shorts, and little hats with feathers in them. They carried big ornate beersteins in their right hands, and sometimes they yodelled. Behind them were their brightly-painted wooden houses, exact copies of the weather-houses and cuckoo-clocks that were made inside them. Heidi and Fritz smiled and smiled in the bright sunshine, and tried to look like reality, in the brightly-coloured posters in the travel agencies all over the world. Their teeth were very white.

The mountains encircled the plain, and between the mountains and the plain were the forests, surrounding it on every side. The forests were very dark, and the trees were fir-trees, immensely tall. It was possible to see only a yard or so into the forest, into the blackness, and there was no grass. It would be terrifying to be lost in that darkness in which nothing grew. The mountains and the plain and the forest were the countryside. At the centre of the plain was the city. Long straight roads converged across the flat bleak plain towards the city. They were not tree-lined. Tree-lined roads were French.

Germany was the city, and the city was called Berlin.

The picture he had in his mind was in black and white. He could not imagine a colour picture of Germany in the 1930s.

'I am sure that he will like Berlin. It's a city made for children.'

That was what Frau Wirth, the baker's wife, had said to Emil's mother, Frau Tischbein, bending over a basin, as she had her hair washed.

'What a din the traffic made! Why, there were streets which are just as brightly lighted at night as during the day.'

The motor cars rushed past the tram honking and squealing, signalling right and left turns, swinging round corners, while other cars followed immediately behind them. How noisy the traffic was! And there were so many people on the pavement as well! And from every side street came delivery vans, tramcars, and double-decker buses! There were newspaper stands at every corner, and wonderful shop windows filled with flowers and fruit, and others filled with books, gold watches, clothes, and silk underwear. And how very, very tall the buildings were.

So this was Berlin.

It had already grown dark. Electric signs flared up everywhere. The elevated railway thundered past. The underground railway rumbled and the noise from the trams and buses and cycles joined together in a wild concert. Dance music was being played in the Café Woerz. The cinemas in the Nollendorf Square began their last performance of the evening. And crowds of people pushed their way into them.

'Berlin is wonderful, of course,' Emil continued, 'but I'm not so sure that I'd like to live here always. Just imagine what would happen to me if I hadn't found all of you, and were quite alone here. It scares me even to think of such a thing.'

As far as the eye could see, the hundred thousand streets and squares of the immense sprawling Baroque city stretched on and on to the horizon in every direction. It was a cold, bleak city, the third largest city on earth, a grey city of stone façades and neo-classical pillars and columns. Massive stone official buildings, bleak, formidable, on a larger than human scale, stretched down broad triumphal ways, their frontages inset with many balconies and steep-set small-paned windows, their surrounds encrusted with curly decorative scrolls and ornate shields, and the figures of gods and goddesses. Wires crossed from side to side of wide boulevards, suspending lamps and traffic-lights, and cables for trolleys. Tramlines stretched away like curves left by skaters in ice, down streets lined with the slim graceful columns of lamp-posts, elaborate filigree metal curls, lamps suspended like pendants from their arched tops. Opera houses, theatres and concert-halls, churches, and government buildings lined the main streets, raising domes, spires, and pillars high into a low sky from which rain was falling.

The great crowds spilled across the streets, beneath the trees and the domes and the spires. The streets were wide and lined with trees, and the crowds thronged them at all hours of the day and night, spilled out of trolley-cars, strode briskly across the tram-lines, passed the packed terraces of outdoor cafés, filled the roads so that only the tops of cars showed, strolled through parks with formal gardens and playing fountains, sheltered from the rain under the trees, as boys in sailor suits watched model yachts on rain-pocked ponds, and nursemaids pushed high-wheeled prams. More and more poured out of Friedrichstrasse Station and the Zoological Gardens Station, their platforms jammed as crowds flooded out of the trains. The four million figures moved down Unter den Linden and Friedrichstrasse, across Potsdamer Platz and the Tiergarten; scurrying across vast squares under umbrellas as the rain poured down; scuttling into shop doorways beneath striped awnings bearing Gothic script; hurrying past huge department stores: Wertheim, Tietz, Karstadt-Haus, KDW; past cylindrical advertising columns and newspaper stands; rushing down wet flights of stone steps into the passages of the underground.

The women wore coats which reached to the middle of their calves, turban-like hats, seamed stockings, and thick fox furs round their necks. The employed men wore dark double-breasted suits with turnups, and no man was bare-headed: they all wore hats, with rims and dark bands. The thousands of unemployed men wore collarless shirts, and caps with large peaks, and moved restlessly amongst the crowds gathering on street-corners, or sat with bowed heads around the edges of the bowls of the fountains. Their backs were turned on the naked marble figures at the centre of the basin, where the waters from the fountain trickled down into the cold marble. All the men were in an identical posture, their faces hidden, heads down and backs bowed, their elbows resting on their knees, and the palms of their hands pressed against their ears, staring down at the ground between their feet, looking as if they were shutting out all the sounds and sights of all there was around

89

them, as if, by not noticing their surroundings, they would not be noticed themselves. Bent over, alone amidst others all the same, the bowed figures concentrated on the rain-darkened ground between their feet, their hands pressed against the sides of their heads, as if shutting out some tremendous sound. Long queues stretched outside the shops, cinemas, and theatres.

Cars were square and sharp-edged, had running-boards, immense mudguards, their large headlamps prominent on either side of heavy radiator grilles. They were soft-topped and open-topped, and had spare wheels in the centre of their boots, seemingly too large, and out of proportion. They pushed slowly through the crowds. Motor-cycles had side-cars, and bicycles were everywhere. Buses with outside stairs, and single-decked trolley-cars moved jerkily between the pedestrians. There were many horses in the streets, and heavy cart-horses drew long carts laden with logs of wood and barrels of beer.

All over the city, thousands of children sat in rigid rows in dark heavy-wood desks, the sort with the seat attached, and an ink-well inset in the top right-hand corner. The windows were high and narrow, above eye-level, and the walls beneath the windows were tiled in browns, creams, and dark greens. White chalk curled in neat Gothic script across the blackboards. The dusty light-shades were at the end of long flexes suspended from high ceilings. The children repeated their nine-times table, phrases from foreign languages, irregular verbs, the dates of wars and battles in which their country had been victorious. Their words echoed in the gloomy interiors. The pens had rusty metal nibs and had to be dipped into the ink-wells after every half-sentence. In every school the hands moved backwards and forwards between the ink-wells and the paper, the hands rose into the air to answer questions, the mouths opened and closed in unison.

Young men and women in knee-length shorts, carrying tall sticks, strode up hills beneath dark fir-trees. Crowds sprawled along the shores of lakes white with the sails of boats, huddled beneath striped umbrellas, eating, sleeping, lying with eyes closed, waiting for the sun. Actresses stood at the tops of steps outside aeroplanes and waved. The planes had propellers and wicker furniture. Pilots had goggles and white silk scarves around their necks. Cigarettes dangled carelessly from the corners of their mouths. Zeppelins slid silently across the skies, half-lost in low cloud, and the crowds in the parks and beside the lakes, looked up and pointed. Vast throngs rotated listlessly in cavernous dance-halls. People fought, outside, in the darkness, in the crowded streets, in the parks, and violence erupted at any time, murders sensational and squalid. Everywhere, there were crippled men with missing arms and legs, supporting themselves on crutches, or pushing themselves along on cut-down perambulators or little wheeled cars, past the middle-aged prostitutes, leaning in groups against the walls, smoking and laughing, their faces thick with make-up.

In hundreds of cheap night-clubs, smelling of stale beer, gloomy with cigarette smoke, down dark stairs from street-level, a young woman wearing a top-hat lounged back on a barrel, leaning to the left. Her right leg, nearer the audience, was drawn up until its heel rested against the knee of her left leg. Her hands were clasped around the raised knee. She was wearing high heels, dark stockings, and a suspender belt, and her short skirt was bunched up around her thighs, her frilled knickers exposed. The expression on her face was mocking, amused, sardonic. Middle-aged men watched her, rapt, awed, aroused, as she lay back, sneering at them. Thin undernourished girls posed naked in shaky tableaux on tiny stages, the beams of the floodlights cloudy with the dust rising from the bare boards beneath their dirty feet, their bodies shiny with sweat, dark hair sprouting in clumps from their arm-pits as they raised their arms. Young men dressed as carefully made-up young women, in filmy billowing dresses, struck poses of immense hauteur, their heads arched back, their profiles sharp, believing themselves to look glamorous and desirable, as they preened, and kissed each other. They were too tall, and their hands were too large, though they painstakingly shaved their jaws and legs.

In dark cluttered rooms all over the city, in the enormous

91

wastelands of tall tenements, the crowded acres behind the public buildings, children, boys and girls with pale and tired faces, lay on unmade beds with dirty sheets, pushed into corners, as foreigners who could not speak German undressed them, and fondled their bodies. They did exactly all that they were told to do. Their faces had the worn, joyless look of people who were hungry and needed money.

In scores of cinemas, vast crowds sat in smoky darkness, and watched impassively as, all across the city, the same images recurred in intensely contrasted black and white in all the films, full of dark shadows, claustrophobic and intensely-enclosed: themes of madness and monsters, unimaginable horror lying just behind the surface of everyday life. A terrifying figure with long hanging fingers and hypnotic eyes lurched across the angled roofs of a stylised city. A city lay deep beneath the surface of the earth, the mindless corridors of an oppressive city of the future, crowded with thousands of dehumanised people moving as one, the buried, submerged workers. A web of electricity created a powerful robot which looked like a beautiful woman. Floods poured down underground passages towards forgotten children, and hands clutched and gesticulated. A monster, made of clay, was brought to life to save a persecuted people. A murderer of children, tracked down through the crowded streets of a great city, his face avid and tortured, was unable to explain what made him do what he had to do, as he moved towards a little girl, who looked up, smiling, towards the unseen killer, his shadow thrown across a poster behind her, in Gothic script, seeking help to trap a murderer. A master criminal held the power of life and death over people who had not even heard of him, as he worked secretly to control the world, altering and controlling the lives of millions. The director of an asylum, controlled by his patients, was hypnotised by an insane man. Dancers moved in geometric patterns, absolutely in step, their bodies used to make a tiny part of a larger design.

The audiences sat and watched as the flickering light from

the screens played on their faces in the smoky halls, now in darkness, now in light.

An image of a man filled the whole screen. The camera looked up at him from below, so that he seemed larger than life, towering upwards like a statue in a temple, to which crowds brought worship and sacrifice. His right arm was raised, rigid, and away from his body, so that the arm, the light behind it, was a dark and solid diagonal across the screen from the top left to the centre. His left hand clasped the heavy square buckle on the thick leather belt around his waist. The knuckles were pronounced in the heavy shadowing of the black and white image. A belt ran diagonally across his chest from his right shoulder, paralleling the dark line of the right arm. Pockets with buttoned flaps were on either side of this belt, to the right and left of his chest, the right pocket slightly raised and puckered by the raising of the arm. His tie, with a tiny knot, was slightly awry. His eyes were in heavy darkness, and the dark moustache, with the shadow from his nose, blotted out the area from the nostrils to below the top lip, like dark blood from a bleeding nose. His neck was in dark shadow, and his ears protruded. He leaned back slightly, to accommodate the balance of his body against the raised arm. He was posed against the sky, and clouds moved behind him, as he stood there, exalted, god-like, carefully posed in this startlingly histrionic position, assuming an expression of stern resolve. Stirring music played, and he stood there, amongst the clouds, greater than life, his shadow immense, his power absolute, his confidence unshakeable, staring into a future which would be of his creation. Nothing else mattered but this.

In front of him, perfectly in line, was a huge contingent of men in black breeches, stripped to the waist. Their stance was relaxed, and their legs at ease, slightly apart, and they were holding spades, their hands resting on the handle at waist-height, the bright metal cutting-edge touching on the ground between their feet. At first, with their naked chests and black breeches, they looked like medieval headsmen holding their

93

axes, all the executioners of history gathered together in one place.

Outside the cinema, the crowds moved up and down the streets of the nation which was a city called Berlin.

The people moved quickly, rather jerkily, slightly blurred, in a grainy scratched atmosphere of black and white, or a smeary sepia, as though everything were discoloured with rolling banks of smoke. The synchronisation was not quite right, and the people seemed to rush headlong down the streets. A voice commented on their actions, rather heavily jocular, or theatrically serious, with a liking for alliteration, stressing every fourth word. The voice spoke English, and was totally devoid of all genuine emotion, as though the people did not matter, were already lost in history. The words were quite separate from the scenes they purported to describe.

A little boy called Emil, wearing his dark blue Sunday suit that his mother cleaned by holding him between her knees and scrubbing with a dampened clothes-brush, and who wanted him to go to a good school, pushed his way through the crowds, holding a suitcase and a bunch of flowers for his aunt, followed by a crowd of children, searching for a thief who had stolen the money that was for his grandmother.

Everyone was gazing into the distance, in silence. Children were carried on their father's shoulders, held by the ankles, gazing into the distance, to where their parents were gazing. The people had strong faces, rosy, tanned by the sun in past years, and hands were held up over eyes screwed up against the falling rain. The reflections of the buildings and the crowds were very distinct on the soaked streets. Their right arms were lifted into the air, at an angle up and away from their bodies, pushing forward against each other, like children keen to answer questions in class, thrusting up their hands – 'Please, sir! Please, sir!' – all those enthusiastic children, desperate for the approval of their watching teacher, who paused, looking out over the class, noticing those who did not know the answer.

The crowds, stretching far away into the distance, wandering aimlessly year after year, had found someone to give their

94

wandering a purpose, to shape them into a pattern, to make all the millions of them a part of history. Their lives did not belong to them any more. Each individual had ceased to exist. The city, crowded with millions of people, had become a dot on a map.

He saw a long line of people stretching away into the distance.

He saw women in calf-length grey overcoats, long dark hair, stumbling forward, holding their children's hands, families trying to cling together, men in dark clothes, heads bowed, carrying suitcases, a long procession, trudging through the snow, unarmed, surrendering. They did not cry, or call for help, but stared with eyes full of all that they had seen. Their eyes were the only part of them he could see. He could never see them clearly. They were always partially hidden by the falling snow, and the barbed wire which surrounded them. As they moved forward, the snow began to fill in their footsteps. Long, sealed trains travelled eastward, through the snow, to unknown destinations, unknown places with strange names, a foreign country a long way from home, an immense and frozen emptiness.

Their names were not known, and everything about them was forgotten. They would die, just like all the others, he had thought, without names, without faces.

Eight

He was at the beginning of a story of which he already knew the ending.

In fairy-tales collected by the Brothers Grimm, the innocent and the pure in heart always seemed to triumph, even after much fear and suffering: Hansel and Gretel always outwitted the witch and escaped, the Seven Little Kids and their mother always destroyed the wolf, the three sisters in *Fitcher's Bird* overcame even death itself to defeat the murdering magician. But he could still remember the mounting desolation with which he read some of the Hans Christian Andersen fairy-tales when he was little. He had read them over and over again, hoping that this time the ending would be a happy ending, but the endings never changed: the little match-girl always died entirely alone, frozen to death on New Year's Eve, surrounded by burned-out matches; the little mermaid always melted into foam, after bearing her suffering bravely; and the steadfast tin soldier and the ballerina always perished in the flames of the stove, leaving only a little tin heart and a metal sequin behind. He had been unable to put them away and forget about them. He had been drawn, compulsively, to read them with engrossed attention, and had wept as he found himself realising what the inevitable and unchanged end of the story was going to be.

It was raining again outside, and the wind blew in strong

gusts. The sea was only a slightly darker grey than the sky, dull, reflectionless, possessed of great depths. The curtainless windows rattled and swam, and the empty playing-fields were drab and distorted. Low black clouds rolled heavily across the sky, like smoke from a burning city.

He looked around the bare white walls of the echoing, bare-boarded bedroom, and thought of Lotte Goetzel, Hedwig Grünbaum, Anna Kahn, Stefanie Peters, and all the other little girls, lying in bed, pictures and postcards on the walls, listening to rain falling, and thinking of their families in Berlin, writing the letters that he was now holding in his hands.

In July, 1938, Lotte Goetzel had rejoined her parents in Berlin, after being at Southwold for two terms, and had not returned to the school.

Berlin-Charlottenburg 2.
9th August 1938.

Dear Mr High,

Growing difficulties make it impossible for us to send our daughter back to Southwold. We have now lost all our business and it is impossible for us to pay the fees any longer. We know no one who can help us. Lotte was very glad to see her family, friends, and her little dog here, but we know she will miss the kindness she was shown in England. She was very unhappy in a strange land sometimes, but we know how much you tried to make her feel 'at home'. We think it, perhaps, was too early to separate the child from home. As she is such a shy, quiet girl, we were really afraid that she felt so homesick so far away from us. You may think this is sentimental in us, but I think, as a father, you will understand our feelings. It would be our wish to give her in your school if we could, but perhaps it was too early. She is only 12.

We are leaving Germany, and going to Holland. I have good hope of a position with a firm in Amsterdam. There is a Jewish school for children from Germany, and we

97

hope to give Lotte a practical education so that she may be able to earn her own money by her hands, wherever she goes, with what the future may bring for us. All our furniture is packed and waiting to be sent away, but we do not know whether it will be possible to take it with us.

We thank you with all our hearts for all you have done for Lotte. She sends a letter for you.

With many good wishes for you and your school,

Peter and Aline Goetzel.

Dear Mr High,

I am so sorry that I did not say goodbye properly to you and Misses High. I was too unsure. Thank you for the nice report.

The sea was rough when we crossed, and most of the passengers were sick. Hanno Weiler and I were not. Hanno looked after me very nicely. His mother and father kindly took me home from Hamburg, on their way back.

I am now hier in our house, and it is going to be sold. It was very exciting to help to get everything ready, and empty all the cupboards. A lot of lovely old things we found, where we never knew from. It was great fun. Grossvater is going to sell his farm and come with us to Holland. It is a big adventure.

Mutti and Vati like the school foto very much. Vati has put it under glass, and all my friends like it.

Love to you and Misses High,

Your affectionate pupil,

Lotte Goetzel.

I send you a foto. Please keep me in good memory.

The little dark-haired girl stood at the edge of an empty field, holding a small Scotch terrier, smiling up at the camera. She wore a headband in her short hair, and was wearing a pinafore dress, with a brooch in the shape of a swan.

In October a postcard had come from the Goetzels, saying

that they were safe in Amsterdam, and that was the last communication the family made with the school.

Anne Frank and her family had been German refugees in Amsterdam.

Some years ago, when they had been in The Netherlands (Jo had been seven, and had told all his friends at school that they were going to Never Never Land) they had visited the Anne Frank house in Amsterdam, where the secret hideout of the Frank family and their friends was preserved, where they had hidden for two years, before being found and sent to Auschwitz and Bergen-Belsen. He had a blurred memory of darkness, and echoing bareness, and above all else, a little section of the wall where the remains of some pictures and postcards stuck there by Anne Frank had been preserved. The memory he retained more than any other was a postcard of Princess Elizabeth and Princess Margaret Rose. That single postcard had brought that dead girl very close to him in that bare room.

In spite of everything she had written, less than three weeks before she and her family were taken away – his father had talked about the visit to the Anne Frank house in a school assembly, and read from her diary – *I still believe that people are really good at heart. I simply can't build up my hopes on a foundation consisting of confusion, misery, and death. I see the world gradually being turned into a wilderness. I hear the ever-approaching thunder, which will destroy us too, I can feel the sufferings of millions and yet, if I look up into the heavens, I think that it will all come right, that this cruelty too will end, and that peace and tranquillity will return again.*

On television, a few weeks ago, a Dutch woman journalist, a sympathiser with Red Phoenix, had been interviewed about her comments on the current trials of terrorists in West Germany (the same terrorists, now imprisoned, for whom Red Phoenix were holding the Berlin schoolchildren hostage), and the interviewer had mentioned Anne Frank's name when the Palestine Liberation Organisation had been mentioned. The woman had laughed, not sarcastically or ironically, but with

99

genuine amusement, and called the diary her 'least favourite work of fiction'. 'This figure of six million dead Jews,' she had said, 'must have been chosen, I suppose, for some cabbalistic significance, and everyone knows it has little basis on factual accuracy. It is a hoax. Surely you have read the books that prove this. It is a fiction sustained by Zionist propaganda to attempt to give some historical justification for the acts of Jewish military aggression against the Palestinian people. Some Jews did die in the war, of course, but so did millions of Poles and Russian civilians – and the figures here are not open to question. People always die in war.' The programme had ended with her laughing face, amused and incredulous at the interviewer's naïvety, like a bright young lawyer defending a war-criminal. When the film of *The Diary of Anne Frank* had been shown on television, all the characters speaking with American accents, a boy in Jo's form had written: 'It was in black and white. It was about a girl who was hidden from the Germans in a small room, and she wrote a diary about it, but at the end the Germans found her and her friends. It was a long film, but there wasn't any fighting in it. It was set in the nineteenth century.'

Always, as he worked through the confused and decimated contents of the files, through 1933, 1934, 1935, 1936, he had been aware of 1939 ahead of him, and of what was to happen in the years that followed. He knew that when one day in 1939 was reached, a door would close forever on these people, and they would never be heard of again. Every hope, comment, and plan expressed within the letters and postcards from Germany had the pitiful inadequacy of humanity caught within the inexorable machine of historical events, too close to the earth to see the pattern that had to be viewed from far above to be recognised. Only the cool eyes of the future historian, dispassionate and distanced, could sift through and find a pattern, like an archaeologist piecing together the broken fragments of bone or pottery in a destroyed and long-forgotten city; and there were fragments, as he moved through the final

100

files of 1939, badly burned many years previously, the remains of photographs, postcards, and letters, blackened and charred at the edges, falling into ash, crumbling away like documents in a tomb exposed to the light of day, the final letters of all those people in Berlin, from Leonie Matthias, Nickolaus Mittler, Mrs Viehmann, and all the others, as the doors closed, one by one.

Mrs Viehmann, the mother of Kurt and Thomas, was one of the parents he had come to know best.

The last letter he had found from her had been posted on 27th June, 1939. It had no address, was typed – all her other letters had been handwritten – and was unsigned. In pencil, Mr High's secretary had written *Mrs Viehmann* at the top.

Dear Mr High,

I am ashamed that it is so very long a time, and we have not written to you, and we wished to do it long ago, but you must certainly know what horrible things have happened here in the time since. I have not told you, but my husband is imprisoned since the 10th November. You will, I think, know the events of that time. I have not told my children, and beg you not to tell them, because they will be so frightened and anxious, that they will not be able to learn anything at school, and it would be of no use to concern them, because they can do nothing at all to help us, as, it seems, I cannot myself. I now type all my letters, and write to both my children in the names of myself and my husband, and so they do not realise what has happened to their father. I want, also, so awfully much the money for the posting. I would be grateful if you could excuse me, that I beg you to give the letter enclosed to my sons.

I would be very happy if you should have the kindness to write to me, and tell me what you think about my children, and how they progress, especially Kurt and his future, as soon he will leave the school. Although we

101

have to live now for the day alone, my husband and I cannot help thinking sometimes of the future. Our children now, even more than before, are all our future, and all that happens there. I have not the hope that we shall be able soon to discuss the matter of Kurt's career with you in England, because even if my husband is free from the prison, and receives a permit for England, then we have to wait for our papers here in Berlin. That will last many months, and we hear so from our friends who try. I have already a permit for domestic work in England, and I do all things possible to deliver my dear husband, but events are stronger than I am.

Kurt, I think, wishes to be a surgeon, but do you think this is possible that he can be educated to a profession, without the money? Rudolf, I know, had to leave school early and begin work of a practical kind, because of the times in which we live. Many years are needed for study. We feel great sorrow that we cannot care for our sons as we would like to do, and must be obliged to ask for the help of friends so many miles away. (Help, dear Mr High, that has been so willingly given to us.) We would be grateful for your advice in this matter. Kurt may have to go to America later, but it may last years since he must wait until his turn.

Thank you for telling me when Thomas was ill. I beg you, when the boy is ill, please continue to let me know. Do not be too careful of me. I am more quiet when I know. Thomas, is still, I think, unhappy in his heart, although he does not say so in his letters. Please forgive him and understand him, Mr High. He is young, but he has known much, the torture of the last years and the separation from his home and his family, the things which hurt us who are grown-up, and even more a child. He has a great need for affection which we gave him with all our hearts when we were with him, and could hold him in our arms. If the noisy and lively surroundings of the other boys, as is usual and natural in a school, seem to make him sad, it is because our house was always quiet, and my son, after all this time, must still remember this. For me, as a mother, it is difficult to ask you to do what I should do myself, but please, Mr High, could you speak kindly to our son so that he may become more cheerful inside? I hope you will be pleased with him. Your last observation in his school report, and the school photograph, filled our hearts with the utmost joy. Our sons are very well-looking, both, and seem so tall.

Thank you for all the good things you do for our boys.

All is incertain, but we look forward impatiently to the chance to come to England, and be with our boys again. We have still hope that the police will return our passports. I hope you and Misses High are in good health.

Excuse me, for troubling you so much.

Affectionately yours,
The mother of the boys
you called 'gifted'.

Throughout July and August, the postcards from Nickolaus Mittler had arrived at the school. Every week, there was a new one, carefully and neatly written, each view on the front chosen to be different.

Berlin-Charlottenburg.
27th June 1939.

Dear Mr High,

Would you be so very kind and write to me what is the matter with the permits for me and my big brother to come to England? Are the applications for the permit in the home office already? I wish to give as little trouble as possible, but I worry because my parents have the mission to come to England, and they wait only for the permits for us.

Yours respectfully,
Nickolaus Mittler.

Berlin-Charlottenburg.
3rd July 1939.

Dear Mr High,

Could you please send me a certificate, stating that you are admitting me and my big brother to your school? The authorities here in Berlin state that we must produce this document to show that we are really going to come to your school, and then they will allow us to have passports. This document must be authenticated in England. Please send this to me signed by the authorised department. Do you need any other documents? We have our photographs, and doctor's certificates.

Yours respectfully,
Nickolaus Mittler.

Berlin-Charlottenburg.
9th July 1939.

Dear Mr High,

Thank you so much for kindly sending me the certificate. The Berlin passport office now says that the certificate must be made out in German, not in English. The passport office also says that your signature must be authenticated by the police of your district. Thank you so much for your trouble. I am sorry to be a nuisance. When we have the permits we will need to wait more weeks before we can get the passports, but we wait hopefully. When we get the passports we will go to the British Passport Central Office for a visa. Then all will be ready to start for England.

Yours respectfully,
Nickolaus Mittler.

Berlin-Charlottenburg.
15th July 1939.

Dear Mr High,

Please would you not be indignant if I once more am

104

compelled to write to you. The British Consulate here requires a letter from you in which you confirm that me and my big brother are to be accepted into your school. The Consulate must know from your letter that a guarantor has been found for the paying of the school fees in England, and then it will grant the permission for us to enter England. I beg you to send me this letter. What cloathings will we need for the school?

Yours respectfully,
Nickolaus Mittler.

Berlin-Charlottenburg.
21st July 1939.

Dear Mr High,

Thank you very much for the letter you kindly sent me. I took the letter to the British Consulate of our city, but I beg to inform you that the letter did not contain the guarantee that someone had been found to pay my fees, and the consulate demands this before it will give permission for us to enter England. What we need is only a form! I shall not forget all your endeavours to help us. I am so sorry to force your amicability so often. I shall try to repay all you are doing when I come to England. We have bought our cloathings ready.

Yours respectfully,
Nickolaus Mittler.

At the end of August 1939, Leonie Matthias, who had written often from Berlin for the Jewish agency 'Elternhilfe für die jüdische Jugend', asking for help for new children, or making enquiries about the progress of children who had been received into the school, had written from a city many hundreds of miles away from Berlin. 'Elternhilfe' had been closed down by the German authorities on November 10th, 1938, and she wrote as a welfare worker in another children's relief organisation.

'Since the events of last November,' she wrote, 'a very large number of Jewish schoolchildren are gathered here, and we are trying, with every means at our disposal, to ensure that there can be some way in which their higher education may continue. They are the future for their parents. Could you possibly agree to accepting a few more children? I would take as much trouble as I did from "Elternhilfe" to ensure that the pupils I recommend to you would fit in well with your school. Please give my best wishes to the children I know in Southwold. Has Stefanie Peters settled in well? I would like to hear how they are all progressing. I had a very nice letter from Kurt Viehmann the other week.

'I hope you do not mind if I enclose a photograph of an eleven-year-old girl, Ruth Martin, an only child whose parents owned a farm in Saxony. Her uncle managed to emigrate to America, and he is trying to raise a financial guarantee for her. Her parents hope to go to America, also, in the near future. She is a very nice, friendly little girl, and I am sure that she will fit in very well. She has started to learn English, and is making good progress.'

Ruth Martin's photograph had been removed from a photograph album. There were little patches of blue paper at each corner where it had been pulled away from the page where it had been glued, and, on the back, someone had written, in pencil: *Unsere Ruth an ihrem elften Geburtstag.*

Everywhere, in the final file, were the photographs of children.

He found himself looking at the photographs, searching for death in the children's faces, afraid of the feelings inside himself, trying not to think of the future, trying not to visualise what he knew was deep inside his head.

From November 1938 onwards, the photographs, letters, and school-reports had flooded into the school in greatly-increased numbers, as parents tried to find somewhere to send their children, far too many of them for it ever to have been possible for more than a very few to have been offered places.

The vanished children smiled in all the photographs, as their parents waited for someone to decide whether they would live or die. Some photographs, like Ruth Martin's, were taken from family albums, others seemed to have been taken specially for the application, the child's eyes showing an awareness that the attractiveness of his smile was the most important thing in the world to his parents.

... These two little boys have all their papers in order, and could leave Berlin immediately, if there were a school available for them in England, and if someone could guarantee their payments for them ... Elise is ready for travelling since a long time, but she is waiting still for her permit from the 'Home Office' ... Sehr geehrter Mr High, Frau Clara Werth gab mir Ihre werte Adresse, da ich beabsichtige, meine Söhne nach England zu geben. Die Jungen sind vor allem in Sport und Musik sehr begabt und singen sehr schön. Meine Kinder sind Halbwaisen, der Vater war Bankvorsteher. Da wir jüdisch sind ... Lucie is thirteen, and can draw nicely, and plays the piano very beautiful. She wishes to be a nurse and help the ill people, because she is a gentle girl who would like that everybody should have his place in the sun. Whatever I say about her, you will say that it is only the mother talking, but I will tell you something of the nature of my little girl so that you may see freely for yourself. One time I brought home Lucie from school, and at the door was a beggar with a child, who, I confess, I did not remark them, but Lucie did. I talked with my friend who was waiting in the house for me, and we was always disturbed by Lucie, who always would try to call me aside, and anger me. I sent her from the room, but when my friend went away, Lucie ran back in and begged for food for the beggar. The beggar was gone away and she returned weeping, and was not to be moved to eat her supper. This is the kind of child she is, and I implore that you will accept her in your school ... I am told that you accept German boys in your school. I have a grandson of fourteen ... Dieter ist ein ausgezeichneter Schüler. Er ist gewandt und mutig und

107

*beweist im sportlichen Kampf Fairness und . . . I am very
sorry to have to tell you that Emmy and Doro Werth were not
evacuated from Germany in time to escape the war. They
were to have come across in a children's transport in the second
week in September in time for the beginning of term. When
we realised how extreme the danger was, it was too late to
advance the date of their leaving, and all the German trains
had been reserved for the exclusive use of troops for days before
the war actually started. Walter, I know, will have realised
that his sisters have not made it in time . . .*

Hand in hand, the little boy and the little girl stood at the
edge of the dark pathless forest, in which the wild animals
were waiting to tear them to pieces. The boy looked back
towards his home, but the adult gripped his arm, and pulled
him away.

He had seen, in school history books, some of the photographs of what had happened within that dark forest, facts to
be learned by children for examination now, like the date of the
Battle of Hastings, and what the Magna Carta was. Before he
moved up from the infants' school to the junior school, he had
decided that the date of the Battle of Hastings, and the meaning of the Magna Carta, were questions that he was bound
to be asked, and he had learned them carefully, confident of
impressing everyone with his erudition. On his first day at
junior school, a teacher had approached him and opened her
mouth. He had thought that the long-awaited moment had
come, and that she was going to ask him for the date of the
Battle of Hastings, but all she had asked him was his name,
and what class he was in. He had sat down in his place and
eagerly awaited the opportunity to answer a question about
the Battle of Hastings or the Magna Carta. Eight years had
passed since then, and he was still waiting for someone to ask
him for the date of the Battle of Hastings. But, even if no one
ever did ask him, he still knew the answer.

The S.S. man stood with his submachine-gun, his face

impassive, a man doing his job, rather bored. The little boy wearing the cloth cap, his short coat reaching to above his knees, stood with his arms in the air, as he had been told, his face frightened and bewildered. He was about six or seven years old. Women and other children were all around him, being rounded-up. A woman just behind him, a young house-wife in a headscarf, holding a heavy bag in her left hand, was only able to lift her right arm in surrender, a band with the Star of David around the top of her arm, like the black band of mourning that people sometimes wore after a death in the family. Beside the little boy was a woman, both hands raised, looking back at the face of the man with the submachine-gun, as if memorising what he looked like. She had a battered zip-up bag over each arm, like the full shopping-bags of a woman returned home to her family in the evening, after taking a bus from the city-centre.

It was a picture he had often studied. There were no bodies, no blood, and only one gun was visible, but to him it was the image of war, the most horrifying photograph he knew of the Second World War. He remembered the Ingmar Bergman film his father had ordered for the Film Society, the two women alone on the lonely island, the nurse and her patient, the actress, who had retreated into total silence, studying that same photograph.

There was a newsagent's shop in Lowestoft where he was not known, and where he always went on his infrequent journeys there on the bus, to go to the cinema, or just to walk around, away from Southwold. The women's magazines, and the comics for children – frames in war comics where immense German soldiers screamed in agony as flames from flame-throwers hit them full in the face, as a grinning British private shouted, *Try that for size, Fritzy!!* – were at the front of the shop, opposite the counter, covers forward on sloping stands. At the back of the shop, in the far corner, where he always went, trying to appear casual and offhand, was the section labelled *Adult publications*. Adult meant sex. Adult meant filth. Adult meant brutality and excitement. That was what being an adult meant.

He stared at the photographs in the magazines he took from the revolving stands, at the genitals of the naked young men to compare them with his own, at the naked women with their legs wide open, pinned out like Biology illustrations – clitoris, vagina – their fingers pushing down on themselves, holding themselves open like imperfectly-healed wounds after an operation. The young men and women thrust out their sexual organs like beggars exhibiting mutilations in exchange for charity.

The same racks which held the pornographic magazines also held the American magazines whose covers had crudely-drawn illustrations of tall S.S. officers beating near-naked women with leather whips, and thick paperbacks about concentration camps and war atrocities. Fascinated, but appalled, avid and disgusted, he gazed at them, unable to avert his eyes, the intensity of his gaze only equalled by the intensity of his gaze between the legs of the naked women in the photographs, their faces contorted into expressions of mock ecstasy, their tongues protruding from the corners of their mouths, like women who had been strangled.

On the outside covers of the paperbacks were reviews from obscure newspapers in American cities, always ending in exclamation marks, always in block capital letters. Inside, he found himself staring absorbedly at the photographs of what lay at the end of those long railway journeys, those many, many trains converging from all over Europe on the concentration camps, and the extermination camps, those places with clumsy, uncouth names far away in the east, in Poland: Majdanek, Treblinka, Chelmno, Sobibor, Belzec, and Auschwitz. With compulsion and dread he stared at the heaped masses of skeletal bodies, long thin arms and legs like the pale twisted roots of heaped and rotting vegetables lying crushed beneath the earth, and brought to light, mouths open as if screaming, stomachs fallen away beneath the jutting rib-cages, the impenetrable thicket of limbs; stared as he turned the

110

books at different angles, trying to recognise human faces, trying to see the expressions on them, the hideous things that had once been men, women, and children.

They had names. They had faces.

He held their letters in his hand, he recognised their handwriting, he knew their names, he saw their faces, he had shared their most private hopes and fears, he knew who had not managed to leave Germany in time. He knew the obscenity that lay ahead for these families, parents and children, walking together hand in hand in that darkness, carrying their possessions in suitcases, and rucksacks from family camping holidays.

Some things were not to be thought of. Some things were not to be endured. In a nearby country, only a few years earlier, in the lifetime of his mother and father, millions of people had been humiliated, robbed, degraded, and murdered, the populations of entire cities. If Hitler had completely succeeded, would the Jewish people have become a lost and legendary race, cloaked in mysteries and myths, like the Babylonians and the Assyrians, as distant and strange as the Old Testament people in an illustrated Children's Bible? Opposite the English translation of *The Children's Haggadah*, sections of the book had been printed in Hebrew script, like the carving of forgotten alphabets on fragments of stone in museums. *This year we sit at the table half glad, half sad, here, far away from our own land; but next year we hope to welcome a joyous Seder in the land of Israel. This year we are still as unhappy as slaves in many countries, but next year we pray to be a free and happy people.*

He had been sitting in the bare room for a long time.

Before he turned the door of the inner room in the bedroom, and turned the key on the returned and neatly-sorted files, he looked at the photograph on the front of the final postcard from Nickolaus Mittler, the sepia faded and cold, as in all the other postcards.

111

Friedrichsbrücke und Nationalgalerie, Berlin. (Friedrich Bridge and National Gallery, Berlin.)

He was looking at a scene which was like a model he had once seen in a museum, a reconstruction of Imperial Rome, stone statues dark against the skyline, naked and draped figures of gods and goddesses, columns and colonnades stretching into the distance. The bridge – the same bridge that had been visible in the distance in the aerial view of the cathedral – crossed the river in three shallow arches, with figures as tall as three-storey houses holding lamps in the shape of torches high into the sky, two on each side of the bridge, above the foundations between the arches. Four tall columns, one at each side of the approach to the bridge, were surmounted by colossal eagles about to soar into flight. Beyond the bridge, on the far side of the river, lining its bank as far as another bridge in the distance, a row of tall columns rose straight up, like an illustration in an art book of the five orders of architecture, shafts, capitals, and architraves enclosing a columned building with a pediment, like the Acropolis or the Capitol, the great national temple, rising above its surroundings, floating above the trees, the columns, and the river. The whole scene was like a triumphal way through a pagan city, along which slaves were to be led into perpetual bondage.

Victory was everywhere in the immense city, stretching away across the plain to the forest and the mountains: on the column in front of the Reichstag, huge, winged, holding aloft a wreath for the victor in her right hand; above the Brandenburg Gate, her chariot rising above Unter den Linden, the trees so large and close together in the tree-filled boulevard that the street seemed like a long narrow park between solid walls of buildings; in the soaring eagles on the Friedrich Bridge: everywhere was victory, victory, victory.

The whole city was depopulated, all its people vanished. There had been no human figure in any of the photographs on the postcards from Nickolaus Mittler. The massive buildings, larger than any human scale, were there for ever, more solid and important than the ephemeral figures, tiny and fragile,

112

of men, women, and children, holding hands to stay together. The streets of the immense deserted city stood out in sharp relief in the cold light of early morning or late winter afternoon. The columns of shadows were long, stretching away and narrowing into the distance.

The same shadows stretched out across the empty playing-fields outside the window.

Scientists had now invented a bomb which could destroy human beings, but leave buildings undamaged. The body's cell-structure disintegrated, the molecules came apart.

Jo's copy of *Emil and the Detectives* was a Thomas Nelson school edition, a reprint of 1942.

The English schoolchildren in their evacuated school read about the adventures of Berlin schoolchildren, as the bombs rained down on Berlin from the English planes. On the Contents list it said *III. The Journey to Berlin Begins: 26.* He thought of the boys in Nollendorf Square, saying goodnight to each other and shaking hands like grown-up men, who are very serious about something.

He had flicked the pages of the book over, and looked at the page open in front of him, the illustration on page 39 of Emil's nightmare on the train, Emil running for his life past the skyscraper two hundred storeys high, pursued by the horses, and the train, and the engine-driver with the whip. *The city was so large, and Emil was so small.*

He wondered whether Emil Tischbein was a Jewish name, and where the little boy from the small country town who loved his widowed mother would have been in 1942. Emil, Mrs Tischbein, Grandmother, Pony Hütchen, Aunt Martha, Uncle Heimbold, Gustav, the Professor, little Tuesday, Gerold, Friedrich the First, Arnold Mittler and his little brother: where would they all have been, what would have happened to them all, caught in the flames as the book burned?

Bent over in the quiet room, Nickolaus Mittler, carefully and painstakingly, wrote at the table near the window, writing the

113

postcards in his best handwriting. He was absorbed like a figure in a Dutch interior, bowed over a letter or a musical instrument, his inner feelings possessing him more completely than his surroundings.

He needed more time.

He needed the future to approach more slowly.

Nine

Beside a dark pathless forest there lived a poor woodcutter with his second wife and his two children, a little boy and a little girl. The boy was called Hansel and the girl Gretel. They had very little to eat, and when a great famine came to the country, the father found it impossible to find them any food at all. One night when the children were in bed, he lay thinking of what he could do for them all. Overcome with fear, he groaned, and said to his wife, 'What can we do? How can we feed our poor children, when we can't even feed ourselves?'

'I know exactly what we can do, husband,' answered the stepmother. 'Tomorrow morning, very early, we will take the children into the midst of the forest, where it is darkest, light a fire for them, give them each one last piece of bread, and then we will go off to work, and leave them there, and never return. They will not be able to find their way home again, and we shall be free of them.'

'No, my wife,' said the father, horrified, 'we cannot do that. I could not bear to leave my poor children alone in the forest. The wild animals will tear them to pieces.'

'Fool!' said the woman. 'If we do not do this, then all four of us will die of hunger. We must destroy them in order to live ourselves. Otherwise you might as well start making the coffins for us all now.'

The man's heart grew heavy, and he would not agree with

her. She did not leave him alone until he had agreed to her plan. He said to himself, 'It is not right,' and yet he agreed.

'I still feel sorry for mý poor children, whatever you say,' said the father.

The two children, tormented by hunger, had been awake all this time, and had heard everything that their father and stepmother had said about them.

Gretel wept bitterly, and said to Hansel, 'They do not want us. We cannot live when we're all alone in the world.'

'Don't be frightened, Gretel,' Hansel said. 'I'll think of a way to save us both. I'll always be here to look after you.'

When the adults were asleep, Hansel got up, put on his coat, and tiptoed downstairs. Very quietly, he opened the front door, and went outside. The moon was shining brightly, and the white pebbles which were scattered on the ground in front of the house glimmered in the moonlight like newly-polished silver coins on the dark earth. Hansel bent down, and began to gather up the pebbles, dropping them into the pockets of his coat until they were both crammed full.

Then he went back into the house, closed the door very quietly, and tiptoed upstairs, where Gretel lay waiting for him, frightened to be alone.

'God will not forsake us,' Hansel said to Gretel. 'Don't believe that we can ever be totally abandoned. Sleep peacefully, my dear little sister.'

They prayed, and then, comforted, they both went to sleep.

Next day, when it was still dark, before the sun had even started to rise, the woman came into the children's bedroom, and woke them up, saying, 'Come on, get up you two! We have to go into the forest to collect some wood for the fire.'

She gave each of them a tiny piece of bread, and said, 'This is the only food that we've got left. Save it for your dinner. If you eat it too soon, you'll have nothing at all to eat later.'

Gretel put both pieces of bread into her pinafore pocket, hers and Hansel's, because Hansel's pockets were filled with the pebbles. Then the whole family began to walk into the darkness of the forest.

When they had walked a little way, Hansel stood still, and looked back towards where their home was. He did this again and again as they walked further into the forest.

'What do you think you're doing?' his father asked him. 'You're holding us all up with your dawdling. What on earth are you looking at?'

'I'm sorry, father,' Hansel said. 'I'm looking back at my little white cat. He's sitting up on the roof, all by himself, looking for me. I never said goodbye to him.'

'Don't be such a fool!' the woman said. 'That's not your little cat. What you can see is the morning sun shining on the chimneys.'

Hansel, however, had not been looking back at his cat, or at the sun shining on the chimneys, but to check that the white pebbles he had been secretly dropping from his pockets had been leaving a track that he would be able to follow back out of the forest.

When they had reached the very middle of the forest, where it was darkest, the father said, 'Now, children, collect up some wood, and I'll light a little fire for you so that you won't be cold.'

Hansel and Gretel worked quietly together, and piled up the pieces of wood they found until they had made a little white hill of dead wood. The father set fire to it, and when the flames were burning very high and very bright, and the shadows were flickering amongst the trees, the woman pretended to smile, and said, 'Now, children, you must be tired. Lie down beside the fire where it's nice and warm, and your father and I will go into the forest and cut a good supply of wood. When we've collected enough, we'll come back for you, and then we can all go home, and sit round a lovely warm fire together.'

The adults went away, and Hansel and Gretel sat together beside the fire. In the middle of the day they ate their little pieces of bread, and, as they could hear what they thought was the sound of an axe nearby, they thought that their father was working only a short distance away from them. It was

117

not an axe, however, but a branch which their father had fastened loosely to a withered tree, tapping backwards and forwards as it was blown by the wind. As Hansel and Gretel sat there in the warmth, listening to the slow tap-tapping coming through the trees, their eyes began to feel heavier and heavier, and they fell into a deep sleep.

When they woke up again, the fire had long ago died out, and it was cold and dark, the deep night fallen all around them in the forest.

Gretel was frightened, and began to cry.

'We will never be able to find our way home,' she sobbed to her brother. 'We're too deep into the forest ever to find our way out.'

Hansel put his arm about her shoulder and comforted her.

'Don't be frightened,' he said. 'Just wait a little while, until the moon has risen, and then we will be able to find our way home. I promise you.'

When the full moon had risen above the trees around them, the white pebbles that Hansel had dropped behind him shone with a cool silvery light. He took his little sister by the hand, talking to her and encouraging her, and then began to follow the trail of pebbles through the forest.

All night long they walked through the forest, guided by the pebbles, and, just as day broke, they once again found themselves at their father's house. They knocked at the door, and the woman opened it. When she saw that it was Hansel and Gretel she disguised her real feelings, and said, 'You've been very naughty and thoughtless! Why did you sleep for so long in the forest? Your father and I were beginning to think that you were never coming back!' The father, however, rejoiced inwardly, because it had almost broken his heart to leave them all alone in the dark forest.

A few months later, there was another great famine in the country, and the children, lying awake in bed, again heard their stepmother talking to their father.

'The only food we have left is half a loaf. When that has gone, it will be the end of us. We must get rid of the children.

118

That is the only possible solution. We must again take them into the middle of the forest, and make sure, this time, that they can't find their way out again. It's the only way we can save ourselves.'

The father was overcome with guilt and grief.

'We cannot do that,' he said, angrily. 'Parents should share their very last mouthful of food with their children. We cannot abandon them.'

The woman would not listen to a word he said, and turned on him furiously, mocking and taunting him.

'Once you have failed to say "No",' she said, 'you can never say "No" again. Because you agreed the first time, you cannot fail to agree with me now.'

She continued to argue with him, until he was compelled, once again, to agree with her.

Hansel waited until the adults were asleep, and, as he had done before, he got up, put on his coat, and tiptoed downstairs. He planned to collect the white pebbles again, and use them on the following day to save them, but it was impossible for him to do this. The woman had locked the door, and he was unable to get out.

He went back upstairs, and explained to Gretel what had happened.

His little sister began to cry, and Hansel tried to console her.

'God will never abandon us,' he said to her. 'Don't cry. Sleep peacefully. We will find a way out of the forest somehow.'

The following morning they were again woken by the woman before the sun had risen, and she pulled them from their beds in the darkness.

The pieces of bread that were given to them were even tinier than those they had had the first time. As they began to make their way into the forest, Hansel, as he had done the previous time, stood still, and looked back towards their home, more and more often as they went deeper into the forest.

'You're slowing us all down, doing that,' his father said. 'Come on, keep up with the rest of us.'

'Sorry,' Hansel said. 'I'm looking back at my little pet

119

pigeon. He's sitting up on the roof, all by himself, looking for me. I never said goodbye to him.'

'You're a fool!' the woman said. 'That's not your little pigeon. All you can see is the morning sun shining on the chimneys.'

Hansel had not been looking back at his pigeon, or at the sun shining on the chimneys. He had been crumbling his piece of bread in his pocket, and secretly dropping crumbs to leave a track that he would be able to follow back out of the forest. Little by little, he dropped all the crumbs, little white fragments on the dark earth.

The woman led the children into the very deepest part of the forest, to a place where they had never been before in their lives. Again, a huge fire was made, and again the woman pretended to smile, and said, 'Now you stay here, children. When you feel tired, have a little sleep. We are going into the forest to cut wood for the fire at home. When we've finished, we'll come back to you in the evening, and take you back home with us.'

The adults went away, leaving the two children sitting beside the fire. When the middle of the day came, Gretel shared her little piece of bread with Hansel, because he had scattered all his bread in the forest. Then they fell asleep, and night fell, but no one came for them.

They awoke, alone, in the deep blackness of the night in the forest.

Hansel again put his arm around his sister to comfort her, because she was afraid of the darkness.

'Don't be frightened,' he said. 'Remember what happened last time? Just wait, and when the moon has risen, we will be able to follow the trail of bread, and reach home safely.'

They waited until the moon had risen above the trees, but there were no crumbs anywhere to guide them through the forest. Thousands of birds flew about the forest during the day, and they had eaten every piece of bread. The whole trail that Hansel had laid so carefully had disappeared.

Hansel took his little sister by the hand.

'Don't worry,' he said. 'I'm sure we'll soon be able to find the way out of the forest.'

But they did not find it. They walked all through the night, and for the whole of the next day, until night fell again, but they were still in the depths of the dark forest, weak and dizzy from hunger, as they had been able to find nothing to eat except two or three berries growing on the ground. Exhausted and cold, unable to walk any further, they huddled together beneath a tree, and fell asleep.

The sun had already risen when they awoke the next morning, and it was now three mornings since they had left their father's house. They began their journeyings again, but seemed to find themselves travelling deeper and deeper into the darkness, across the black earth on which no grass grew. Hansel began to realise that they would soon die of hunger and exhaustion, and he was wondering what he could say to his little sister.

At midday, when the pale sun was visible in the sky above the trees, a lovely snow-white bird, bright against the dark trees, sat on a branch just above them, and sang so beautifully that they stood still and rapt, drinking in its song, as if to fill the hunger that was inside them. When it had finished singing, it spread its wings, and flew a short distance away from them, alighting on another tree. They walked towards it, hand in hand, stumbling and faint, Hansel helping Gretel, longing to hear that sweet music once again, and, as they drew near, the bird spread its wings again, flying just ahead of them, staying just in sight. All that afternoon, the two children followed the white bird through the forest, until, as night fell, they reached a little clearing, and the bird flew on to the roof of a little house in the centre of the clearing, and stayed there.

It was a lovely little steep-roofed house, standing amidst the trees in the quiet forest, in the cold clear air, surrounded by lawns and flower-beds, with soft warm light glowing out of its windows to guide them towards it in the rapidly-falling darkness. As they came closer up to the house, they saw that it was built entirely of gingerbread, covered with little decorated

121

biscuits, and that the windows were made of clear sugar, shining with a soft translucent glow. It was a dream come true.

'Look, Gretel,' Hansel said, 'our prayers are answered. We have found something to eat at last. I will reach up and eat a bit of the roof, and you can eat some of the window. It will taste nice and sweet.'

Hansel stood up on tip-toe and broke off a little corner of the roof to see what it tasted like, and Gretel leant against the window, and pulled away a piece of the pane.

Faint with hunger, they were feasting on the house, when a soft little voice cried out from inside:

'Nibble, nibble, gnaw,
Who is nibbling at my little house?'

The children thought quickly, and then answered:

'The wind, the wind,
The heaven-born wind,'

and went on eating, not pausing for a moment. Hansel, in his hunger, tore away a great chunk of the roof, and Gretel pulled out a complete circular window-pane, sitting down and leaning against the wall to eat it.

Suddenly, the door of the house opened, and a very old lady, frail, bent-over, came out slowly, supporting herself on crutches. Hansel and Gretel, frightened and guilty, dropped what they had in their hands, and Hansel put his arms around his sister.

The old lady, however, smiled gently, and held out her arms.

'Oh, you poor, dear children,' she said tenderly, 'here in the forest all by yourselves. You must come in and let me look after you in my house. Here you will be safe. Here you will be cared for.'

She took them both by the hand, and led them into her little house, talking to them kindly, and welcoming them. She sat them at the table in the little kitchen, beside the warm firelight, near a big tiled oven, and the smell of cooking filled the room. Then she set a meal before them: milk and pancakes, with sugar, apples, and nuts. Afterwards, she took them into the bedroom, where two pretty little beds were covered with soft

122

white linen. Hansel and Gretel lay down to go to sleep, and
thought they were in heaven.

The old lady had only pretended to be kind. She was, in
reality, an evil witch who lay in wait for children, and who
had built the little gingerbread house in order to lure them
into her power. When she had a child under her control, she
killed it, cooked it, and ate it, and that day was a feast day
for her. Witches have red eyes, and cannot see far, but they
have a keen sense of smell, like animals, and know when human-
beings are nearby. When she realised that Hansel and Gretel
were drawing near to her house, she laughed with malicious
delight, and said, 'I shall have them! They shall never escape
from here.'

Early the next morning, before the children were awake,
she got up and went into their bedroom, and looked at them
as they lay asleep in bed, young and unprotected, with their
rosy cheeks, and warm breath, their hands flung back against
their pillows.

'These two will taste good!' she thought, drooling.

She seized Hansel, sleepy and confused, in her shrivelled
hands, and carried him behind the house into a little stable,
and locked him into a cage made out of iron bars. Hansel
screamed repeatedly for help, but there was no one there to
hear him, or to come to his help. The immense dark forest
stretched away on all sides, silent and unpopulated, empty
of all humanity. Snow had started to fall, and the huge flakes
fell silently from the grey sky, covering all the dark earth with
a deep, trackless whiteness, dazzling to look at.

The old woman went back into the bedroom, and shook
Gretel until she woke up.

'Where is Hansel?' Gretel asked at once, frightened to be
alone. 'Where is my big brother?'

The woman laughed, immensely amused.

'You're never going to see him again,' she said. 'Get up!
Make yourself useful. Bring me some water from the well, and
then you can cook something good for your brother. I have
locked him in the stable behind the house, and I'm going to

123

feed him up and make him fat. When he is all ready, I am going to eat him.'

Gretel, terrified and lonely, sobbed as if her heart would break, but the old woman only laughed at her, and tormented her, and forced her to do all that she had commanded.

In the days that followed, as the snow continued to fall, all the best food was cooked for Hansel, locked away out of sight in the stable, but Gretel got nothing to eat but the shells of crabs. As she worked, weak and exhausted, beaten and mocked by the old woman, she found a long corridor leading out of the kitchen, near the oven, lined with doors. Behind the doors were many rooms piled to the ceilings with all kinds of goods, all neatly stacked and sorted. One room was full of money, paper and coins from many different countries; another was full of jewellery, rings, brooches, necklaces, valuables of every type imaginable. There were rooms entirely filled with children's clothing, with shoes, with children's toys, underclothing, blankets, handkerchiefs, and hair cut from girls' heads.

Every morning, the woman went out to the little stable, and up to the cage.

'Hansel,' she commanded, 'put your finger out so that I can feel if you are getting any fatter.'

Hansel, thinking desperately, stretched out a little bone through the bars of the cage towards her, and the woman, whose eyes were dim, thought that it was Hansel's finger, and was angry and astonished that he seemed to be getting no fatter.

Four weeks went by in this way, and Hansel still seemed to remain as thin as ever, so that the woman was seized with impatience, and decided that she was not prepared to wait any longer.

'Gretel!' she shouted at the little girl. 'Bring me some water this instant. I've waited long enough. Tomorrow, whatever happens, I'm going to kill your brother, fat or thin, and cook him.'

Almost blinded with tears, Gretel stumbled towards the well, the water falling unheeded from her eyes. She tried to remember what her brother had said to her, to comfort her, when he was there beside her, and could speak to her, and give her courage. 'God will not forsake us,' he had said. 'Don't believe that we can ever be totally abandoned.'

'Dear God, please help us,' she cried in her despair. 'If the wild animals in the forest had torn us to pieces, at least we would have died together. I'm so frightened of being all by myself.'

'Stop that noise!' the woman sneered. 'It won't do any good at all. No one can hear you, and no one will come and help you. Your brother dies tomorrow.'

Early the next morning, when it was still dark, the woman made Gretel get up, light the fire, and hang up the cauldron full of water. Outside the windows, the snow was still falling.

'We will bake first,' the woman said. 'I've already heated the oven, and the dough is all kneaded and ready.'

Gretel stood bowed over the cauldron, silent, the tears running down her cheeks.

'Come here,' the woman said. 'Stand in front of me.'

Gretel did as she was told, too frightened to resist without her brother.

'Take off your clothes,' the woman said.

Sobbing helplessly, frightened and alone, Gretel took off her shoes, her pinafore, her dress, and all her clothes, folding them neatly as she undressed, as she had been shown by her mother before she died.

When she was completely undressed, the woman took a pair of scissors, and cut off all Gretel's hair, close to her skull. Gretel remained with her head bowed, as her hair fell to the floor, the braids falling all in one piece, with a ribbon still in them.

'Give me that chain,' the woman said.

Gretel unclasped the chain from round her neck. It had been a birthday present from Hansel, and had a little star at the end of it. She handed it to the woman.

She took Gretel over to the oven, from which the flames were already darting.

'Creep in,' said the woman, 'and see if it is properly heated for the bread.'

'Hansel,' Gretel whispered. 'Hansel.'

'Get in,' the woman said, and Gretel, without saying another word, climbed up into the oven, and the woman shut the iron door, and fastened the bolt.

When she was sure that Gretel had been burnt to death, the woman went behind the house, and walked through the deep drifts of snow to the little stable, and walked up towards the iron cage where Hansel was imprisoned.

'Gretel?' Hansel called out when he heard someone approaching. 'Is that you, little sister?'

'Your sister is dead,' the woman said. 'I put her into my oven, and she was burnt to death. Now it is time for you to die.'

She opened the door of the cage.

'Get out,' she said. 'What are you crying for?'

Hansel stood shivering in the cold stable, his breath white. The whole stable was flooded with a hard bright light from the snow outside.

'Come here,' the woman said. 'Stand in front of me, and take off your clothes.'

Shivering, in tears, Hansel fumbled with the fastenings of his clothes, folding them neatly as he took them off, as Gretel had.

When he was completely undressed, Hansel stood shivering helplessly, his hands cupped in front of him, his head bowed, his body pinched and white.

'Give me that ring,' the woman said.

Hansel pulled at the ring until it came away from his finger, and handed it to the woman. His mother had given it to him on the day that Gretel was born, and told him that it was a present brought for him by his new little sister.

The woman took Hansel out of the stable, and into the deep snow.

'Walk to the house,' she said.

His arms wrapped around himself, his body burning in the

126

icy air, the flakes of snow like drops of fire, Hansel walked naked through the falling snow in the dark air. He saw the thick smoke pouring from the chimneys of the house.

'God, do not forsake me,' he whispered. 'Let my little sister be alive. Don't let me die.'

She took Hansel over to the oven, where the flames were now high and bright.

'Get in,' the woman said. Hansel stood for a moment, and saw his sister's hair lying on the kitchen floor, beside her neatly-folded clothes. Then, without another word, he bent over, and climbed into the oven, and the woman shut the iron door, and fastened the bolt.

When she was sure that Hansel was dead also, the woman went back out of the house, and to the stable. She closed the door of the iron cage, and picked up Hansel's clothes, then walked back to the house, closing the stable door behind her. The whole clearing around the house was white and trackless as the snow continued to fall.

Inside the house, she picked up Gretel's clothes, and added the children's clothes to all the others in the room in the corridor. She put Gretel's chain and Hansel's ring in the room with all the other jewellery, and then walked back into the kitchen, and towards the oven, drooling with anticipation. Today was going to be a feast day.

She is living there still, happy and contented, living in perfect comfort and prosperity, waiting for the children who come through the forest.

Ten

He turned at the top of the steps, and stood looking back the way he had come, towards The Ferry House, out into the darkness of the playing-fields, from the terrace that ran along the back of the school-buildings, above flood-level. As he looked, for a long time, out across the low-lying fields towards Dunwich, down the coast, he felt, in the darkness and cold air, as if he were at the edge of the earth, facing out across the unknown, at unmapped and desolate regions stretching endlessly away, the sound of the sea on his left. He had felt the same feeling when he was little, when he stood outside the front of The Ferry House, outside the school grounds, and looked across the common, rising beyond the footpath, filling all the distance to the sky. It had seemed to him like the beginnings of the outside world, a mysterious and untracked wilderness where the sun went down, and strange creatures lurked in the bushes and long grass.

He turned, and walked towards the school, the unlighted mass of the buildings a darker solid shape against the sky. He was not a boarder in the school, and only saw the dormitories during the holidays. In his imagination, they were always empty and echoing, the beds stripped, and the walls bare.

Instead of walking along the terrace to make his way out on to Dunwich Green, near Tennyson's, he went inside, switching his torch on as he opened the nearest door, and began to walk parallel to the terrace, through the centre of the buildings.

The reflection of his own light moved towards him, caught in the glass of classroom doors. In the school theatre the set was still up for *The Winter's Tale*, the tall leafless tree in the centre, its branches spreading over the bare stage, and there was one of the programmes designed for them by Lilli, still lying on the floor, a dusty footprint across its front cover.

His feet echoing, he passed empty classrooms, with writing still on the blackboards, possessions stacked neatly in the lockers, all the children gone. The room he eventually went into was the German room, where he had hardly ever been before, as he did not take German. He switched on the light, and sat at a desk near the door, at the back of the room.

Above the blackboard were tables of the definite and indefinite articles, irregular verbs, personal pronouns. Lotte Goetzel's father had written that Lotte felt very strange when she heard English parents calling their children 'you', because she thought that was really a plural pronoun, and it sounded so formal and distant. The days of the week, and the months of the year, written in German, which lined the walls near the ceiling, reminded him of the letters of the alphabet which ran around the walls in his infants' school, when there had been so much to learn, so many tasks to master, in order to become grown-up, a big boy: weeing like a big boy, and climbing the stairs properly, having a proper big boy's bed, tying a tie, fastening shoe-laces. Every child, through all the years of childhood, worked with great intentness to acquire all the skills of a proper adult person.

On the blackboard was a partially-erased drawing of a human figure, a clownish matchstick giant drawn by a small child, the parts of the body carefully labelled: *das Auge, der Mund, das Ohr, die Nase*, and he saw that every object in the room had a neat little label on it, naming what it was, as if giving that object reality: *der Stuhl, der Tisch, die Decke, die Tür, das Fenster*. When he had been teaching Lilli, over a year ago, he had drawn blank maps of parts of Southwold, and simplified sketch outlines of some of her illustrations, asking her to write in the names of as many of the buildings or objects as she could. He remembered her clutching her pencil fiercely, her eyes determined.

The vocabulary list pinned to the wall beside the blackboard was for *die Stadt: the town,* and the first words in the list which followed – *die Hauptstrasse: the main street, die Strasse: the street, die Gasse: the lane –* reminded him of the nursery-rhyme on one of the birthday cards from Jo. (*This is the key of the kingdom: In that kingdom is a city, In that city is a town, In that town there is a street, In that street there winds a lane . . .*)

Jo had bought two cards for him, one for a ten-year-old, and one for a six-year-old, and he had found them suspended from the ceiling above his bed when he had woken up that morning, together with a poster – *Happy Birthday, big 16-year-old-type Corrie –* that he had drawn using his set of Winsor and Newton coloured inks that had been one of Lilli's Christmas presents to him. He loved the decorative boxes that the bottles of ink came in. The one he liked best was the design for Ultramarine ink, where a little boy in a sailor-suit knelt on a rock at the edge of the sea, sailing a model yacht. It was like the design on the painted enamel egg in the kitchen. Each of the cards had Jo's signature inside, and a pencilled scrawl that was Matthias's signature when Jo held his hand. All that it said inside the card for the ten-year-old was *I can do anything, now that I'm ten.* He remembered how much he had looked forward to his tenth birthday, because his age would be in double figures.

As a small child he had hated having his birthday so close to Christmas. It had seemed so unfair and profligate to have two such special days so close together, reducing the time he could spend on speculation and building up excitement, though his parents had always been meticulous in keeping the two occasions quite separate, giving his birthday an importance not overshadowed by Christmas. He had still not shaken off the slightly resentful feeling that a birthday only three days after Christmas was not really a very well thought-out birthday. He remembered asking his mother why she hadn't chosen him on a better day. He had hankered after October 28th at one time, as something to look forward to in the middle of the longest term of the school year. Birthdays belonged to dark nights and cold weather: the games inside could be more exciting then, he had thought.

When he walked through into the sun-lounge from Lilli's kitchen, she was bent over her loom, on the far side. He had heard the click-click as he approached.

She moved to one side of the bench as he came in, and he sat beside her.

They sat in silence, side by side, as they often did for a while before he went to bed. He leaned forward, watching the pattern emerge, thread by thread. He looked carefully at the design of the shawl she was making. Lilli's hands moved smoothly backwards and forwards, up and down, the hand nearest to him passing the shuttle swiftly away from him.

As he had requested, he had had no formal celebration for his birthday: Lilli had baked a cake, Sal had come round, there had been presents, but that had been all. He would open his presents at supper-time, the last thing before he went to bed. It was a tradition he had started when he was little, to keep his birthday presents as far away as possible from his Christmas presents. After Matthias had gone to bed they had played Dungeons and Dragons for a time, though Sal had had to leave before the game was completed.

'Twenty questions,' Corrie said.

' "Try to speak. Try to answer without writing anything down," ' Lilli quoted to him.

'What is your name?'

'What is the name of my school?'

'What is the weather like today?'

'What season is it?'

'How old am I?'

'What part did Jo play in *The Winter's Tale*?'

'Which room are we in?'

131

'Don't ask me what Pieter's job is, will you?' Lilli asked eventually, when the questions had started to become more and more bizarre.

He had been reminding Lilli of some of his early lessons with her, when he had completed his hour with her by firing twenty questions, trying to get her to answer automatically without the agonies of thought, insisting on complete sentences. He used to hold gently on to her hands, and not allow her to move them, so that she could make no gesture, no movement to convey the words she could not speak or think of. She had been unable to think of the word for 'headmaster', and, although he had included the same question over and over again, she had been able to think of no other word for Pieter's job than 'big teacher' for several weeks.

'You were a very hard teacher,' Lilli said, smiling.

'Inevitably, with such a troublesome pupil. I had to complain to the big teacher.'

He remembered how, in his early lessons, he had been self-conscious, not fully at ease, and sometimes found it difficult to talk beyond the words he had prepared for the lessons with her. He had used an awkward jocularity, copied from some of his teachers, unsure of how to communicate with him. He had become the teacher, and all his experience up to that time had been of being taught.

They sat together in silence again.

He remembered how the skin of Lilli's hands felt loose, as if flesh and bone beneath were too small for it, like something soft and yielding to lie against if you were tired.

'You look very thoughtful,' Lilli said, some time later.

It was the usual invitation to talk.

'Not really.'

'Yes, really. You've been the same all week, Corrie. Worried about the onset of old age?'

'It's just some music I'm trying to . . .'

'Yes. You have been practising a lot recently.'

There was a faintly interrogative note in Lilli's comment.

He couldn't tell Lilli what his main thoughts were about,

132

that inner room in the bedroom, that entry into the forest, pathless, grassless, black as perpetual night within a few feet of the edge.

'Jo's very unhappy at the moment, Corrie. I think he's been lonely, and wanting to talk to you. He says you've been locking yourself in The Ferry House, and staying there all day.' Lilli paused. 'And he hasn't heard any music from inside.'

'I've been thinking.'

'He was crying last night. It's the end of the year. The time when you look back.'

'Mum?'

'Yes.'

'He was very quiet when Sal was here.'

Corrie thought for a moment.

'You're right about the end of the year. I don't feel that time has passed, just because I've had my birthday today, but on New Year's Eve I'll be thinking of a whole year that's gone.'

'He's missing her very badly just now. Christmas, and Pieter being away.'

'Do you think the school *will* have to close in a year or so?'

'We're not really supposed to know about that possibility.'

'Jo put his present in the middle of his room, so it'll be the first thing he sees when he gets back.'

They had bought Pieter a piece of Staffordshire pottery when Sal had taken them into Norwich, a ship called *The Three Brothers*.

'He's been upset about that school, and the terrorists as well.'

That afternoon, the terrorists had set a deadline. They were going to shoot one child every half-hour, beginning at ten-fifteen, English time, that evening, and continue until they got what they wanted. That afternoon, on the radio, they had listened to the serious, impassioned voices speaking in German, and then the reporter in Berlin translating what was being said, the telephone line crackling, breathing and heart-beats magnified by the recording. The news-reader's calm, steady voice had mentioned that there was some movement of army units in the area around the school, and then gone on to other

133

items of news: the murder of a kidnap victim in Turin, an explosion in a Paris shopping-centre, the trial of an Arab gunman in London. He had thought of the young woman reading the evening news on the television, carefully made-up, cool, distant, speaking of death and terrorism in a voice that was already the voice of history, unemotional, factual, serious, but controlled. The Red Phoenix terrorists might have claimed to be atheists and members of the extreme Left, but they possessed an impeccable knowledge of the Christian calendar in their choice of date for beginning to kill the children.

'It's a quarter to ten. Let's have supper soon.'

'I'll go and get Jo.'

'Will you talk to him, Corrie? Brothers should help each other.'

He nodded.

There seemed to be no one in Tennyson's when he walked through. Baskerville stood up as he went into their part of the sun-lounge, to investigate who was there, peering closely at him, and then went back to his basket, wagging his tail and looking vaguely gratified after Corrie had scratched his head for him.

He looked out across the Green as he drew the curtains. The lights around the horse-chestnut tree were switched on, swaying in the wind. Two boys were riding bicycles round the tree, their backs to their handlebars, facing out across the saddles, moving their feet round and round backwards, skidding on the wet grass.

He picked up a book lying on the back of the chesterfield, and began to look at the illustrations. He could hear music from Jo's bedroom upstairs. Pooh and Piglet walked through the snow together. Pooh and Tigger sat at a table eating honey. Piglet planted a haycorn. Eeyore, with immense dignity, floated out from under the bridge during the game of Poohsticks. Jo had once written an essay in which he had called Eeyore his favourite character in fiction.

He looked at the picture of Piglet's ears streaming behind

134

him like banners, and then walked out into the hall, to call upstairs.

'Jo?'

He began to walk up the stairs in the darkness.

'Jo?'

The words from the *Saint Matthew Passion* filled the staircase, the whole of the quiet house. The voice soared.

> *Erbarme dich, mein Gott,*
> *Um meiner Zähren willen;*
> *Schaue hier, Herz und Auge*
> *Weint vor dir bitterlich.*
> *Erbarme dich!*

It was an aria which always filled him with emotion and made him feel close to tears, like the moment in the film of *Le Grand Meaulnes* when Meaulnes clutched his baby daughter in his arms, sobbing at the death of his young wife, or the moment in the film of *Romeo and Juliet* when Juliet kissed the dead Romeo, and cried, 'Thy lips are warm.' He was tender-hearted. He was easily moved. He had fought to control his tears when the Film Society had shown those two films, been unable to speak afterwards, moved by the death of children.

There was no one in Jo's bedroom.

He looked at the Advent Calendar from one of Jo's old ladies.

It was a picture of a city in the east, to which kings with gifts were riding. Flat-topped roofs, and battlemented towers rose into the night sky from which a bright star was shining, a light to illuminate the whole of the city and its crowded streets, long ago. Tree-covered hills rose to the distant dark mass of mountains, beyond a lake on whose deserted shore fishing-boats were drawn up in a line. Every morning, from the first of December, Matthias had come into Jo's room very early, to open one of the twenty-four little doors in that city, to reveal the secret scene inside, and woken up Jo to tell him what that day's scene was. The calendar hung in front of the light on the wall, so that Jo could see it as he lay in bed, and so that the light would glow through the scenes behind the little doors, all of which were now open, revealing angels rejoicing, birds in the sky, fish in the lake, families sitting at meals together, musical instruments, cattle and donkeys in the stable. On the morning of Christmas Eve, Matthias had opened the last little door, the most elaborate and beautiful of all the pictures. In the warm candle-lit interior, the young mother gazed lovingly at the baby who was born to die.

It was a German Advent Calendar, printed in Munich.

> *Erbarme dich, mein Gott,*
> *Um meiner Zähren willen.*

On December 18th Matthias had woken Jo to tell him that that morning's picture was of a radiator. Baffled, Jo had got out of bed to investigate, and found that the illustration was of a harp.

He saw the wet footprints on the carpet, leading away from the record-player, and followed them through into the bathroom, putting on the light in the corridor.

Jo was sitting in the bath.

Corrie sat on the lid of the lavatory pedestal, and leaned back, stretching his legs out.

'I shall avert my eyes if my presence is inhibiting your performance,' Jo said. He had a very crisp, clear voice. Judith had told him he spoke 'very good English'.

The light was not switched on, and Jo's skin looked very white, and faintly gleaming in the light that shone through the open door from the corridor.

As Corrie watched, Jo closed his eyes, held his head very upright, and shook it very rapidly from side to side, a gesture he often made, so that his hair would fall neatly into place.

He moved across, and sat on the edge of the bath.

Jo was not having a bath. His chest was bare, but he was dressed in the jeans that Sal had bought him for Christmas, and sitting in the half-filled bath to shrink them to size. He was peering closely at a book. There was a carton of yoghurt standing in the soap-rack. The water was already a deep shade of blue.

'How long have you been in there?'

'An hour or so.' He spoke very quietly, his voice expressionless.

He put the book on the soap-rack, picked up the yoghurt, made little finicky movements with the spoon. One of Matthias's rubber ducks was floating in the water beside him.

'I think it's about time you got out, then. That water's cold, Jo.'

His skin was very white, cold, and rough with goose-pimples.

Corrie began to speak with the dead-pan elocution of a lesson in a foreign language, pointing as he spoke.

'The water. The Johann. The chest. The asthma.'

'The cough. The guts. The floor,' Jo said. 'I'll be alright.'

He was very sensible about his asthma usually, and knew when to ask for his tablets, and when to go to bed.

Jo looked at him.

'Any more news about that school?'

'No. Nothing new.'

'What do you think will happen?'

He looked very intently at Corrie.

'The troops will go in, like they did with that plane. There's nothing else that can happen, is there?'

'They said they'll kill those children.'

'No one was hurt in the plane.'

The terrorists had made no concessions at all. They had severely injured a teacher and a child when they had first attacked the school, and had refused to allow any medical assistance to enter the school. The two had bled to death, and their bodies had been thrown from the windows. They were still there, at the front of the school – no one being allowed to approach near enough to remove them – together with the body of the first person who had died, a teacher who had been helping children out of a first-floor window when the attack had started. Her body lay on the snow-covered grass, where she had fallen from the window when she was shot, a middle-aged woman in a neat grey suit, her spectacles lying on the path to one side of her. They had stared at the picture on the television when the news of the attack on the school was

137

first broken, like people in a passing car looking at an accident in which they were not involved.

There were five terrorists in the school, three men and two women. They wanted eleven members of the Movement Eighteenth October freed from prisons in West Germany, each to be given DM120,000 and flown to a country of their choice. These were the demands they had been making from the very first day of the siege.

He could feel the edge of the bath through his jeans.

'That water *is* cold, Jo.'

Corrie stood up, and held out his hands. Jo gave him the empty yoghurt carton, and the book.

'Thank you, my good man.'

'Out of the bath, grandad, before you shrink away completely. There's not much left now.'

'What time is it, infant?'

Jo's wrist was bare.

Corrie looked at his watch.

'The big hand's on nine, and the little hand's nearly on ten. Lilli's offering supper.'

Jo stood up, and pulled the plug out. He crossed his arms over his chest, shivering.

'O.K.?'

Jo nodded.

'I want to see the news on T.V.'

The chain Jo was wearing round his neck had been sent to him by one of his old ladies. Over three years ago, when Mum had been heavily pregnant with Matthias, they had all appeared on television in a national family quiz programme. They had lasted for several weeks, and got as far as the quarter-finals, losing on the last question, when Pieter had said that 'All the world's a stage' was a speech from *Twelfth Night*. (He had wailed immediately he had said it, but the answer stood.) They had ostracised him for a week until he had begged for mercy, and come down to breakfast one morning dressed in a sack, with some burnt twigs balanced on his head because he couldn't find any ashes. Jo had received fan-mail from half the old

138

ladies in England after their appearances on television, and he had written back to them all. He still received Christmas and birthday cards from them.

'What's wrong, Jo?'

Jo began to take his jeans off.

'Nothing.'

He could feel Jo's pain inside himself. He remembered when he had been very small, it may even have been before Jo was born, and he had been stung many times after blundering into a wasps' nest on the common. He could remember being beside himself with pain and panic, a pain too large and overwhelming for his body to be able to cope with it, so that he had curled up on the floor, whimpering, 'Make it go away, make it go away,' over and over again, hands half-raised as if to push the world away, his body rolling from side to side, and Mum had been there to make the pain go away.

'I'm the one who's known to be moody, aren't I?'

' "He never says a word," ' Jo quoted. He had overheard two girls discussing Corrie in the High Street.

Corrie had never seen anyone with such thin legs as his brother. Jo, seeing Corrie looking at him, struck a few he-man poses, flexing his biceps, his face quite expressionless.

'Are you thinking about those terrorists?'

'No. Well, not really.'

'Are you thinking about Mum again?'

Jo arranged his jeans very carefully on the rail that overhung the bath, aligning the edges precisely, his back to Corrie. He concentrated very intently on adjusting the jeans exactly as he wanted them. It was a while before he answered.

'A bit,' he said eventually, his voice indistinct.

They were Levi jeans. Corrie looked at them, rather than Jo's thin bent back. He felt envious of Cato, who would always have little orange tags bearing his name sewn into the seams of the clothes he wore.

'Corrie?'

He couldn't see Jo's face properly, bent over in the dim light in the corner.

'Mmm?'

'Do you think that Matty remembers Mum? Do you think he still misses her?'

Corrie sat back on the lid of the lavatory pedestal.

'He cried a lot when she first left for Rome. He cried a lot at first.' Corrie paused, trying to sort his ideas out clearly. 'I think, to Matty, she just went away on a journey one day, and didn't come back.'

'But she promised him she'd come back. Does he think she's a liar? Does he think she's just left him? Remember how he kept asking when she was coming back?'

Jo turned.

'Do you still miss Mum?' he asked, looking directly at Corrie.

'Yes, of course I do.'

'I thought it was just me.'

Jo had been the one who had cried. Corrie remembered sitting beside him, with his arm around him, comforting him, very pale in a new suit that was too big for him.

Jo pulled the towel around his shoulders, and they walked through into Jo's bedroom.

The record had come to an end, and Jo switched the record-player off. He awkwardly hitched at the towel, trying to stop it from falling off, as he slid the record back into its cover, and then placed it in the box.

'When Mum had that operation, she would have known if it was very serious, wouldn't she?'

'It was serious,' Corrie answered, and then told Jo something he had never told him before. 'The day before she went into hospital, I heard her crying in the bedroom. I'd come home because Chris's car had broken down. She'd closed the door, but I heard her.'

'Did you go in to her?'

'No. I didn't know what to do.'

He had been twelve, Jo eight.

'She talked to me, the morning before she went.' Jo was sitting on his bed, drying between his toes. 'She was listening

140

to the *Saint Matthew Passion* when I came in. I was upset because she was going, and she said to me . . .' he concentrated carefully '. . . "If you want me to be there with you, play this music, and I will be there. If you want to think of me, think of me when you hear this music." ' He smiled, as he looked across at Corrie. 'That's how the records got so scratched. I used to put one of them on, and sit here with my eyes closed when no one else was there.'

'She told me to look after you when she wasn't there.'

'Remember when I was younger, and you used to come in and sit on my bed when I was scared of the dark? You're my big brother!'

'Little though I am.'

When he was younger, Jo had been frightened of going to sleep. He didn't understand where he went when he was asleep. He had told Corrie nothing about the nightmares he had been having, apart from saying that they were about darkness.

Jo stood up, and walked across to the map of Rousseau.

'In the dark and pathless forest.'

'In the cold, sharp, shifting scree.'

'In the moonless, starless silence.'

'The Journey to the Inmost Sea.'

'Tell me about Rousseau, Corrie.'

'Rousseau is an island, and only we, amongst the non-Rousseaunians know about it. Far away from the rest of the world, inaccessible, and impossible to find . . .'

Jo slowly dressed, listening as Corrie spoke. His T-shirt was an old and faded one, with a large smiling face on the front, like the one he drew inside the letter 'o' of his name: the two dots, and the curve for the smile.

He shook his hair into place, then opened the wardrobe.

'Your present,' he said, holding out a parcel he picked up from inside. 'Nearly time to open it. Let's go to supper. How do you feel, on this, your special day?'

'Older.'

'Well, you are pretty ancient now.'

'Could you help me down the steps, young man?'

Jo gave Corrie his arm, and he began to stagger slowly towards the stairs, miming advanced decrepitude.

Eleven

Lilli came through into their living-room when Jo switched on for the ten o'clock news.

It wasn't until the newscaster had briefly added further details to earlier news stories of the day – the search for the murderers of the Turin kidnap victim, the latest casualty figures in the Paris bomb explosion – that they realised what was going to happen. The frightened child's face appeared again at the back of the newscaster, and the words *School Siege: Day Eleven*, and then, abruptly, the picture on the television screen was the front of the West Berlin school, the three-storey bulk across the snow-covered field, from where the children's voices had come on Christmas Eve, singing *Der Tannenbaum*.

The news-programme was being transmitted live from West Berlin, and a reporter wearing a heavy overcoat stood in front of the camera, holding a microphone. There was noise all around him, a distant siren, a crowd in the distance, and floodlights now illuminated the whole area in front of the school. The reporter kept glancing around him as he spoke.

There was one thing different about the front of the actual school building.

The last time they had seen that building, every window had been dark, the whole of the school looking empty and uninhabited, but now one window, in the middle of the second storey, was brightly illuminated. The zoom-lens of the camera

143

moved rapidly in on this window. In the centre of the window, sitting on an upright school chair raised up so that she was fully visible above the sill, a little dark-haired girl, her hair in plaits, faced out across the newly-fallen snow on the empty field.

It was ten minutes past ten. Almost half-an-hour ago the lights had been switched on in that room to show the girl sitting there. She was the first child who was going to be shot by the terrorists. Just visible at the edge of the window, on the girl's right, was the figure of a woman with a gun. She had been described as 'a girl of 28' in some of the newspapers. Some women could be described as 'girls' at the age of 40, but Corrie doubted that this woman of 28 could accurately be described as a 'girl'. Her most recent act, before the attack on the school, had been the shooting of a West German politician's elderly invalid mother in her bed.

As the time moved nearer to quarter past the hour, the reporter gradually stopped talking, and the sounds all around him stilled. The whole area in front of the school suddenly became absolutely silent.

Corrie realised what was happening.

They were waiting for the sound of the gun.

Sharp, in the silence, was the sound of the window in the illuminated room being opened outwards.

The little girl's face, in grainy close-up, was in the centre of the television screen, blurring, moving in and out of focus as the cameraman tried to get the sharpest possible image.

'No,' Jo said, beginning to get up. 'They're going to show it happening.'

Suddenly, the camera jerked upwards, and all the lights in that area went out, inside and outside the school. There were screams from the unseen crowd behind the camera, a high-pitched shriek of metal as the microphone hit against something, and then there was a brilliantly bright explosion on the roof of the school, and the sound of gunfire from inside the building. There was total confusion, the sound of glass

144

smashing, many voices shouting out harshly in the darkness, lit by the lurid flare.

The camera righted itself, and flames were gushing out from a window on the top floor of the school. The reporter talked rapidly, excitedly. Figures ran in front of the camera, in the flickering light from the fire. Something fell from a window.

There was a lull in the noise and movement, and then the doors at the front of the school were flung open, and children came running out across the snow.

There was further confusion, the sound of a child's name being called over and over again, but the siege was over.

Towards the end of the news, the reporter said that it was believed that three terrorists, four children, and two soldiers were dead. One of the terrorists had been blown up by his own hand-grenade.

'Good,' Jo said, with great viciousness. 'Serves the bugger right.'

Corrie and Lilli looked at each other, and then at Jo. He covered his face with his hands, and then turned to press himself in against the back of the chesterfield, drawing his knees up towards his chest.

In the studio, as the programme was ending, the newscaster picked up a late item of news.

'Reports are coming in,' he began, 'of an attack on an Israeli airliner at Heathrow Airport.'

Lilli's was the last present he opened. He opened it very carefully, trying not to tear the paper. She always wrapped her gifts beautifully.

They had carried supper through into the dining-room, clearing the game of Dungeons and Dragons from the table. The remains of Corrie's birthday cake were still in the centre of the table, and the fir-tree in the corner of the room.

They were sitting in the same places as on Christmas Eve, and Lilli was sitting opposite him, Jo beside him. Just before he lifted the final sheet of paper away, he looked up at her.

145

He thought he knew what the present was going to be. She was looking at him very intently, almost nervously.

' "You look very thoughtful," ' Jo quoted, looking at her closely.

'I've been keeping something secret from you all,' she said.

Corrie looked around for a gap amongst the paintings on the wall, but he couldn't see one. When the final sheet of paper was pulled away, he looked at the glazed painting for a long time in silence, his emotions confused, struggling not to smile broadly, like someone modest who has been extravagantly praised in public.

It was a new painting by Lilli.

Jo bent over beside him, and they studied the water-colour together, the size of a double-page spread in a book.

It was a painting of Corrie doing his prep at the kitchen table during the powercuts in January. In the soft glow of the candles he was facing straight out of the picture, his face rapt, as if committing the words of a play or a poem to memory, books and papers scattered on the table in front of him. The dresser was behind him, and every detail of the room around him was minutely recorded: the wooden weather-house, the Blue Denmark crockery, *The Wind in the Willows* calendar, the chiming pendulum clock, the enamel advertising sign for St Bruno tobacco, the flowers in the Victorian jug, the Droste's cocoa tins, the Pears' soap advertisement, the pine plate-rack, the blue and white pottery village made by Mum on the top shelf of the dresser. The detail was so fine that he recognised the individual designs on the miniature Kate Greenaway playing-cards on the fridge door. The illustration on the Queen of Hearts card was for *I had a little husband*. A little girl stood at a table beside an open window. On the table were two jugs, and a tiny figure of a man dressed in the scarlet tunic of a soldier. His eyes returned to the figure of himself, at one side of the painting, the intensely-realised interior, looking out at anyone looking at the picture. It was like looking into a miniature mirror into his own face.

Corrie doing homework was pencilled at the bottom, and

the signature was *Lilli Danielsohn*, the name of a woman from forty years ago. For a moment he felt that he was looking back into the past, into the face of a boy from long ago who was himself. As he looked, he saw the face of the second sister in *Fitcher's Bird*, the face of a girl who was about his age, her face absorbed and inward-looking, although her eyes looked out of the picture, the face of a girl intent upon making lace, reading a letter, playing a piece of music. Lilli's draughtsmanship was as pure as when she was producing her early work in the 1920s, the colours as delicate, the details as finely-observed.

'It's me,' was all he could say, quietly.

Lilli looked around at the paintings which lined the walls.

'It's so long since I painted,' she said. 'I was frightened I wouldn't be able to do it. I wanted to produce paintings like the work I did in Germany all those years ago.'

'It's just the same,' Corrie said. 'I feel as if I've been given a gift of a famous painting from a museum. I feel like someone special.'

'You are someone special. You're my grandson.'

'Painting*s*?' Jo said, looking up, smiling. 'You said painting*s*.'

Lilli looked at them both, her blue eyes very intense.

'I have painted other pictures. I'm painting still. I feel as though it's all starting to come back to me.'

'When?' Jo asked, interested and excited. 'You haven't said a word about it to anyone. Have you?'

Lilli shook her head.

'No. This is the first one I've shown to anyone. I've been keeping secrets.'

She stood up.

'Come with me.'

She moved to the door, beckoning them towards her.

'Magical revelations?' Jo asked.

Lilli smiled.

'These are my hoards of precious stones.'

They went into the hall, and through into the living-room at the back of the house, where she made them go into the room in front of her, before she switched on the light, and remained near the door, as they moved inside.

The room was still uncarpeted, and the furniture covered with dust-sheets, but Lilli's easel and painting materials stood in the centre of the room, with a paint-covered smock hanging from the side, and, all round the wall at eye-level, unglazed, the heavy paper pinned directly against the wall, were at least twenty water-colours – the room seemed full of them – so rich and intricate that they seemed to nourish the sense of sight, and they were all full of their family, and their home.

Lilli and Matthias sat side by side at the loom, absorbed and bent over together, looking at the pattern as it began to emerge. A view of the back of Tennyson's was from the edge of the low cliff, looking through the burial-ground, as the family sat around on the lawn in summer sunshine, reading and talking around a picnic meal. The whole of the length of the sun-lounge was shown on a cloudy afternoon, with the connecting door open, Matthias painting at the table in the far part and Baskerville lying asleep in his basket amongst the scattered toys. He, Jo, and Matthias stood at the edge of the sea, on the beach just beyond the end of the garden, Matthias holding his hand, and about to throw a twig into the water, for Baskerville. Mum and Matthias bent over a picture-book in Matthias's bedroom, beside the open window. Mum and Judith held a sheet between them in the garden, beginning to fold it inwards towards each other, as Matthias, through the open window of the kitchen, knelt at a chair up against the sink, washing yoghurt cartons for Lilli's seedlings. Mum, Pieter, Jo and Matthias sat around the breakfast table on a Sunday morning, as he adjusted the weights of the pendulum clock, as he did every Sunday morning. The Ferry House was viewed across the playing-fields in autumn, with himself just visible bent over his cello in the upper window, and Jo walking away, with Baskerville at the end of a lead. Mum and Pieter sat listening to music, tired, at the end of the day, in the living-room, books put on one side, the curtains drawn back from the window, the evening sky across the Green. The

148

transient moments of a family in its home, absorbed in the everyday tasks of living and being together, were recorded and given permanence in the paintings which lined the walls, small-scale, intense, deply-felt.

'This will be your birthday present,' Lilli said to Jo, coming up behind them, and they looked at a painting of Jo asleep in bed, the bedclothes twisted around him, the books scattered on the floor, the photographs, maps, and posters lining the walls.

They were the first words anyone had spoken since they first came into the room. Corrie and Jo had moved slowly and absorbedly from painting to painting, not looking at each other.

They stood, finally, in front of the painting that was still on the easel.

It was a painting of the Victorian Evening, the moment just before Mum and Jo had started to sing *Won't You Buy My Pretty Flowers?* Pieter was just looking across from the piano at him, as he prepared to play the first notes on the cello. In the light from the oil-lamp, in front of the scrap-screen, Mum and Jo held their sheets of music, and looked straight ahead towards the spectator, their faces very serious, beginning to draw in their breath before the opening words.

'This is for Pieter,' Lilli said. 'It is the scene I tried to paint first, but I have only now completed it.'

They gazed deeply into a scene that already lay within their minds, like memory given form.

'When did you paint them all?'

Jo's eyes had not left the painting as he asked the question.

'I made my first attempt on the day of your mother's funeral, Jo,' Lilli said, quiet, matter-of-fact. 'They were not paintings, just pencilled sketches. I wanted to draw some of the scenes I remembered with Margaret when they were vivid in my mind. I did not wish to mourn. I wished to remember the happiness in her life. I had wanted to draw for months before that, when I was still affected by the stroke, and, of

149

course, I could not write down the pictures that were in my head. My hands worked against me.'

She turned towards Corrie.

'The very first picture I completed – I had abandoned many others – was the one of you, Corrie, doing your home-work. When I saw you in January, in the candlelight, the scene stayed in my mind. It brought back memories to me that I realised no longer gave me pain, and it was a scene, even then, at that time, I wanted to record. I painted that picture in May. Then all the other pictures came.'

They walked back through into the dining-room, and sat around the fire, as they had done on Christmas Eve, before they opened the presents. Imperceptibly, they had drifted into the mood of their weekly teas together, when they had started to talk seriously to each other.

'I wanted to see whether I still had the skill. I destroyed so much of what I did at first, but I was determined. I would begin to paint again. It made me fight the effects of the stroke more than anything else. Nothing would stop me from begin-ning to paint again. You used to describe scenes for me to draw in your lessons, Corrie, last year, as I began to improve. You were helping me to begin again, although you didn't realise. This Easter, I knew I would begin to paint again, though I had told myself when I left Germany that I never would, ever again. In February I had a letter from an art gallery in West Berlin, asking whether I would be able to help the director there, who was hoping to hold an exhibition of my work. They had collected first editions of all my books, and had tracked down some proofs that still existed, and had an almost complete survey of all my work. They asked if I would be willing to loan them any letters, or documents, or original paintings. I wrote back to him, and said that I had all my paintings, and that I would be happy for them to be on show again, for the people to look at them in the city where they were painted. I laid down some conditions of the way in which the exhibition had to be arranged.'

They looked at all the paintings on the walls around them.

She turned to them both, one after the other.

'I hope you will loan me your paintings – the English ones and the German ones – for the exhibition. They belong to you, now, but I would like all the paintings to be together this one time in Berlin.'

She indicated Corrie's birthday present on the table.

'The exhibition is to be next year, and the arrangements have now nearly all been made, but when the letter came in February I thought, "Could I paint anything now, to add to my German paintings, to show that I am not like someone who died forty years ago? Could I show that Lilli Danielsohn is still alive, still capable of painting?" So, in the way I told you, I began to paint. In the sun-lounge, in the morning light, when you were all out, or at school, I began to paint. I hid everything like a thief. At first I was afraid I would produce nothing I would like to show people, but when I painted the picture of you in the candlelight, Corrie, I was happy. That was the scene I had inside my head that I wanted to show to other people. And so I painted more. Then there were the designs and posters for *The Winter's Tale*. I had become a painter again, and I wished to show my family to other people who had never known them, as I had done before.'

She stood up, opened the door of a cupboard against the wall, near the fir-tree, and took out a large framed photograph. She held the photograph so that they couldn't see it, looking at it closely.

'This photograph must be at the centre of the exhibition in Berlin,' she said. 'It contains the source of all my paintings.'

She began to talk to them, quietly and simply, all that she and Grandpa Michael had kept between themselves, the events that had destroyed her world.

She had come from a wealthy and cultured Dresden family. Her grandfather – Jakob Mitscherlich – had owned the biggest toyshop in the city, in Prager Strasse, the main shopping street. Her father, a university professor, specialising in German Literature, had been wounded, and decorated, in the First World War, and her mother had been a fashionable children's doctor. It was a large and loving household – she had two sisters and three brothers – surrounded by children, nieces and nephews, cousins, aunts and uncles, grandparents. In the early 1920s, a young woman, she had gone to Berlin, and achieved her great successes with her paintings, until the rise of the Nazis had made her and her family *Untermenschen*, sub-humans, and therefore disgusting. All the apparatus had swung into action against the millions of people who had no rights to be treated as human beings, intensifying as the years went by. Friends, who were able to, began to leave the country, but her parents had decided to stay. Germany was their home. Most of her family, those who wished to leave, were trapped, unable to leave children, or possessions, or sick or elderly relatives, or unable to get them out of the country. Her family persuaded her that she ought to leave the country, when she had been given the opportunity of doing so after the events of *Kristallnacht*, when synagogues and houses burned, and the broken glass from Jewish homes and shops littered the streets throughout Germany. She had left for England to work as a domestic servant – she knew no one in England, and her work had not been published there – carrying her paintings and sketch-books, and with her parents' wedding-rings hidden inside a wooden toy, a little doll's cradle, that had once been in her grandfather's shop, before it was taken away from him. Germany was famous for its beautiful children's toys. She never saw any of her family again. They were lost in the immense, crowded darkness, women and children, enemies of the Reich.

When she had finished talking, quietly, without bitterness, she handed the photograph to them.

'This is my family,' she said, 'the family I had forty years ago.'

There was no one he could recognise in the photograph as being Lilli, so she must have held the camera. They were all looking towards her.

Lilli began to identify for them who the people were.

The room in which they sat was the same room as the one

152

in the painting of the christening scene in *Godfather Death*. The same pattern to the plate, the same candlesticks, the same design on the silver, every painstaking detail of the painting. The scene was at a long polished table illuminated by candlelight, just before a meal was about to begin. The family – Lilli's parents and grandparents, her sisters and brothers, their sons and daughters, aunts, uncles, cousins, from the very elderly to a small baby – sat around the beautifully laid and decorated table, formal, consciously posed, everyone very still and serious, looking towards the camera. It was like a small ceremony for a leavetaking or a scene of private mourning, where the emotions could be gentle and low-key.

The second sister from the painting for *Fitcher's Bird* sat half-way down the right-hand side of the table in a simple white dress, her arm around a boy of about five standing beside her, very upright in a dark suit, with a small girl, fair-haired, sitting on her knee. It was Lilli's youngest sister, Edda, and her two children, Florian and Dorothea, the Hansel and Gretel from the painting in his bedroom.

Lilli's sister was several years older in the photograph than in the painting, but completely recognisable. All around the table were the faces from the paintings: The Goose Girl, Rapunzel, The Girl Without Hands, The Fisherman and His Wife, Cinderella, the brother and sister from *The Juniper Tree*, The Poor Boy in the Grave, Snow White. Lilli's family were the people in her paintings; their houses, rooms, and gardens were the places these people inhabited. All around them in the dining-room were the people and places of Lilli's memories of her family. There were 27 people in the photograph.

He looked at the interiors of the pictures in the room around him, and thought of those in the empty room next door, rooms in which families sat quietly together, the doors closed against the outside world, a world which would force open those doors, and destroy all that it found inside, after it had taken what it wanted, the silly family jokes of ordinary people, the schoolbooks lying on the table, the unfinished knitting beside the chair, the photographs and pictures on the walls, the letters

153

hidden away in drawers: all the noise and fury of the world reduced to the grief of individuals, families reaching out their arms, trying to hold on to each other: Pieter and Aline Goetzel and their daughter Lotte with her school photograph under glass and her notepaper with the elaborate letter 'C' for Charlotte; the parents of Hanno and Hedwig Grünbaum, Ruth and Bernhard; Rudolf Seidemann's family; Ernst and Madeleine Jacoby, who had hoped their plan of emigrating to America would work, and their three children, Eugenie, Julius, and Lisette; Walter Werth's mother Clara, and his twin sisters Emmy and Doro who sent him drawings of scenes from home so he wouldn't be homesick; Stefanie Peter's parents, and her little brother, who had just learned how to walk; Leonie Matthias; Nickolaus Mittler, his big brother, and his parents; Kurt and Thomas Viehmann's parents, Katherina and Wilhelm, and the rest of their family; the scores of others, all the family of his grandmother, all the people in all those pictures, the tiny few of the hundreds and thousands of families, all those millions of people, every one a person with memories and individuality, in every one of whom the world existed, like all the people in the book that Jo had been reading in the bath, the visitor's book from the living-room at Tennyson's that Mum had started years ago, with the dark green cover and *Unsere Gäste* embossed on it in gold.

Aidan, Eleanor, Lincoln and Michael came to stay. House in chaos, but cuisine of usual high standard. Jo not quite walking yet.

Lovely gossipy evening. Music, singing, and talk. Michael and Lilli.

Safety note: don't sneeze in the sun-lounge. Michael.

Champagne to celebrate Pieter and Margaret's fourteenth wedding-anniversary. Questionable vintage, but a very jolly body, but enough of Margaret. The champagne was splendid, too. Margaret, I love you! For God's sake push Pieter under a bus! Chris.

They've papered the walls at last. Max.

Now we are five. Welcome to our house, Matthias, from Pieter, Margaret, Corrie, and Jo.

Dropped in for coffee – stayed for tea! Sal.

Lilli's with us now.

Cadged another tea. Sal.

An evening of Bach from the Musical Meeuwissens. Margaret's pregnant AGAIN! Look out the London Philharmonic! Sal and Lilli.

Jo spoke first.

'Did Sal tell you that story about those hostages in Greece during the war?' he asked.

Corrie shook his head.

'A few years ago, before the divorce, she was on holiday with Chris in northern Greece. It was a very remote area, and, during the war, the Germans hadn't occupied it, so it became a centre for the guerrillas. One day the guerrillas made an attack and killed several Germans. The local commander was so angry that he took his troops to the nearest village, and gathered all the villagers together. He told them what had happened, and said, as a reprisal, that one male member of each household would be executed on the following morning. He told them to go home, and decide amongst themselves who was going to be the one to die in their household.'

'What happened?'

'The following morning, the chosen hostages were all killed.'

He thought about the quiet talking into the early hours of the morning, deciding who was to be chosen to die. Who had they chosen? Newly-born babies who had only been alive for a few days, and weak, old men, towards the end of their lives? He imagined them, walking, or being carried, towards their deaths, followed by their grieving families.

Whoever had a child, whoever had a mother or a father, whoever had a friend, whoever was capable of feeling love, of forming a tie, of wishing to protect or care for another person, had a weakness that could be exploited, had a hostage in his life, someone he would give all he had in the world to protect from harm. The cold, the calculating, the political extremists,

155

could plan all their acts upon this sure assumption, and they would continue to have their victories as long as parents continued to have children.

'On Christmas Eve,' Jo said, 'when you were reading *The Wolf and the Seven Little Kids* to Matty, Corrie and I were sitting on the stairs listening.'

Jo looked at Lilli, his face very serious.

'The bit I always remember best in that story is the bit when the wolf goes to the miller and tells him to throw flour over his paws to disguise them.' He began to quote from the story. ' "The miller thought to himself, 'The wolf is going to harm someone,' and refused to do as he was told. Then the wolf said, 'If you do not do as I tell you, I will kill you.' The miller was afraid, and did as he was told, and threw the flour over the wolf's paws until they were white. This is what mankind is like." '

He repeated the final sentence.

'This is what mankind is like.'

Lilli thought about what Jo had said. As she began to speak, her German accent, as sometimes happened when she spoke for a long time, became more and more pronounced as she went on.

'I suppose I should say something wise, something forgiving and fine to teach you all the goodness in mankind, but I have never been one of those people who believes that those who have suffered experience wisdom as an inevitable result of their suffering, become wiser and richer people. 'Suffering' sounds a grand word, as if I were someone special, someone who deserved a special hearing when opinions are expressed, but it is the word which truly expresses the feelings I had. I could never submit humbly in the face of the 'inscrutable will' of a God who had a purpose for a chosen people in which all things that happened played a part. I raged when I was eleven, and my oldest brother's baby died of a simple childhood illness. I raged when I was sixteen, and my old aunt went blind. Why should a baby die? Why should an old woman go blind?

'We were never a religious family. My mother and father

were very modern in their outlook, freethinkers. We were like a Christian family who are Christian only in remembering a little special celebration at Easter or Christmas, but for whom the idea of Christianity played no conscious part in everyday life. I think it might have helped if we had been religious: we would have known that we had something that we felt we were ennobled by suffering for. I could, perhaps, have rejoiced at such a death, going to see the unknown face of my certain God. But the faces I wanted to see were not unknown faces: they were the faces I already knew the best in all the world. We felt like people who were persecuted for being Christians, when we knew nothing of what being a Christian meant, because a distant relation, of whom we knew nothing, lit a candle in a church once, a long time ago. We were Germans, ordinary people, and then they told us that we weren't Germans, we were Jews. It would be like being told that you were no longer regarded as being English because you were a Christian, as if the one cancelled out the other.

'I shall never forget the grief and anger of what I saw and heard in those years in Berlin before I left, and I can never forget what happened to all those I loved. It would be a betrayal to forget them. All my love was with them, and I felt that my love died when they died. No one had the right to expect me to be wise and noble and understanding when they died, and died in such a way. I wanted to kill the whole world. If I had believed there could be a God who had allowed all that to happen to serve His purpose, a cleansing fire from which the world would emerge clean and ennobled as if by a flood, I would have hunted God down and destroyed Him.'

She quoted Jo's words.

'*This is what mankind is like*. Yes, I thought all mankind was worthy of contempt for what had happened, and the cleansing flood has brought filth and fear into every person's life.

'It is a Jewish custom, I think – this is something I have read, not something I have done or experienced: Jewishness is not something I know a great deal about – to leave a pebble

157

at the graveside when you have visited the grave of someone you have loved, someone you love still, to show that you have been there, and remembered him.'

Lilli thought for a moment, and then continued.

'My family, I think, died in Auchswitz, after being in Theresienstadt, some of them, and I know no graves at which I could lay a pebble, but I think of the Polish memorial for the dead on the site of Treblinka. I have seen a photograph in a book: the little area where one million people were put to death. Flat fields surrounded by evergreen trees are there, and thousands of pebbles, stones, and rocks sweep through the fields in broad paths. Each pebble is not a person. Each pebble is a village, each stone a town, each rock a city, and their sizes show the numbers brought there to that place to be killed, from the villages, towns, and cities of Europe, all those men, women, and children, rich and poor, all those different languages converging on a tiny remote place in Poland. In the centre of the fields and all the stones and pebbles, is a rock like a mountain: the stone for all the people brought there from Warsaw to be killed, one third of all the people in that city. I think of all those empty houses, all those deserted streets.

'I felt that the wolf was knocking at the door, and I had no stones to sew inside him. I wanted him to come through the door and destroy me, also. I felt that I could never find any stones: there is only sand in a desert. But, in time, I did find pebbles to lay beside their graves, and tiny pebbles mount up until they outweigh all the boulders you can find at the edge of a mountain. Instead of turning all my heart to stone, the pebbles sank all my bitterness, and I remembered the good things with happiness.'

She turned to Corrie.

'Look again at the photograph. Do you notice anything about it?'

He answered at once, without even looking at the photograph.

'It's the same room as in *Godfather Death*.'

'Yes, but there's more than that. Look at the plate in the

158

centre, near the front. Look at the knives and forks. Think of your birthday cake.'

He looked at the plate in the photograph, and then went back over to the table, carrying the photograph with him, and sat down.

It was the same plate in the photograph as the plate on which his birthday cake stood, the plate that had been used for the Hansel and Gretel gingerbread house on Christmas Eve. The knives and forks they had used on Christmas Eve had been the knives and forks in the photograph, with the letter 'D' engraved upon them in elaborate script.

'As things got worse for my family in Germany, they arranged to hide some of their possessions with friends who lived in the same street, a Christian family. Each night the neighbours came over with their baby granddaughter in her pram, and smuggled things back into their house in the pram, and hid them in one of their cellars. At the end of the war, a letter reached me from Germany, the first letter I had seen with a German stamp since the last letter I received from my mother. It was from the daughter of the woman with the pram, telling me she had possessions which were mine, kept safely for me. She and her husband and daughter came over to England to stay with Michael and me, and brought them with her. She told me that her mother had died in a concentration camp. She had spoken out against what was happening. She, with other Christians, had tried to help, tried to resist what was going on around them. *This is what mankind is like*, Jo. There was a pebble there. I have the plates and the silver, and some of my mother's jewellery and I know of people who tried to stop what was happening in their street. They belonged to no organisation. They were just our neighbours, saying that something was wrong and should not happen, and some of them died for believing this. God would spare a city for one righteous man, but there were many little candle-flames in all that darkness.'

She picked up a book lying on the table beside her chair. It

159

was *Children's Voices*, the new English edition of *Kinder-stimmen*.

'One of the poems in this book, the very first one I illustrated, is by a Jewish woman poet from Berlin. She taught deaf and dumb children. She was taken to Theresienstadt at about the same time as my family, and then to one of the camps, and killed. I don't know, no one knows, when exactly she was killed, or where. She was taken to the concentration camp because she refused to leave her father when he was taken away. He was 80 years old. Her love for her father overcame everything else. *This is what mankind is like.* There was another pebble there.'

She turned the pages in the book, until she was looking at the final poem.

'Will you sing *Auf meines Kindes Tod* again for me, Jo, just as you did on Christmas Eve? The tune is so beautiful.'

Jo looked at Corrie.

'My cello's in The Ferry House.'

'I'll sing it unaccompanied then.'

He stood up, and sang, his voice very true and piercing, the words that Corrie had set to music for *Hansel and Gretel*.

'Von fern die Uhren schlagen,
Es ist schon tiefe Nacht . . .'

'Do you know what the title of the poem means, Jo?' Lilli asked, when he had finished.

'*On the Death of my Child.*'

'Do you know the meaning, word by word, of what you sang?'

Jo shook his head.

'Corrie wanted me to learn the German version for you. I only had a German edition to learn all the words. He explained what the poem was about. We looked at the painting.'

He indicated the painting of the empty cradle on the wall opposite where he stood, the man and the woman sitting opposite each other on either side of the fire.

'It is a poem I often thought about when I was first in England. I had put all my illustrations away. When I looked

160

at the empty cradle in my painting, I had thought of the little empty cradle I had brought with me out of Germany, the little children's toy.'

She looked across at Corrie.

'Corrie knows exactly what the words mean. He has read the English translation. His music fits the mood so exactly, and he has been able to express the emotions of other people. Listen, Jo, these are the words for which Corrie wrote the music.'

Holding *Children's Voices*, she read the translation, slowly and quietly, the words that went with the music Corrie had written for the song in *Hansel and Gretel*, the song for Florian and Dorothea Weisser.

> 'The clock strikes far away,
> It is already deep in the night,
> The lamp burns dimly,
> Your cot is made.
>
> Only the winds still go on
> Keening round the house.
> We sit lonely inside
> And often listen out.
>
> It is as though you were
> Going to tap gently at the door,
> As if you had only lost your way
> And were coming back tired.
>
> We poor foolish people!
> It is *we* who are still wandering,
> Lost in the horror of darkness –
> You have long ago found your way home.'

She passed the book over to Jo.

'They are beautiful words, and you wrote beautiful music, Corrie, but now it is only the first three verses that remain

161

true for me. I cannot agree that death is where a child belongs, that a child is best out of the world, that death is the most comforting home for a child. We *are* wandering, we *are* lost in darkness, perhaps, in England, in Germany, over much of the world, but it is the children who will lead us out of this darkness, who will put an end to our wandering. With each child's birth, they say, the world begins again, and it is you who must use your life in trying to find a way, trying to light that darkness. This is what I truly believe.'

She turned towards Jo.

'Will you sing again for me, Jo, in English this time?'

Corrie was still sitting at the table.

As Jo sang, he looked at the painting of himself in the candlelight, and the candlelight of the photograph, all Lilli's family grouped around the table at the beginning of a meal. In *Godfather Death* the poor man had refused to allow God to hold his child as His godson at its christening, because God left the poor to starve; rejected the Devil because he led men into evil; and chose Death as his child's godfather, because Death made all men equal, and made no distinction between rich and poor. When his godson was grown up, Godfather Death led him deep into the forest and gave him his present, the skills which would make him a rich and famous physician: a secret herb to cure ills, and the power of telling if a person was going to live or going to die. Whenever the godson was with a patient, Godfather Death would appear, and if he stood by the patient's head, he would recover, but if he stood by the patient's feet, that person belonged to Death, and the godson was forbidden to use the herb to cure him. At the end of the story, after the godson had defied Death to save the life of a king's dying daughter, Death took the young man deep below the surface of the earth into a cave where countless candles burned, millions upon millions of them, flickering, rising up, and dying away perpetually, the lights of the lives of all the people in the world, and showed him the candle of his own life, tiny and guttering, and, when the young man pleaded with him to light a new candle for him, out of love, so that he could marry the king's daughter, and live the rest of his life in happiness, Godfather Death threw the little piece of candle down to the floor of the cave, so that it was extinguished, and the young man belonged in the hands of Death for ever.

He remembered the candles of his birthday cake, and of Christmas Eve, when the fir-tree had been covered with candles, and the whole room swayed and swam with their flames. That was how they had staged the final scene of *The Winter's Tale*. Leontes, Perdita, Paulina, and Polixenes had moved silently towards the statue of Hermione in the chapel, hardly visible in the dark centre of the stage, beneath the white wood of the dying tree, behind the banks of unlit candles, and, in a long sequence without any dialogue, as his music was played by the consort offstage, as Jo began to sing, they had taken tapers, knelt before the statue of the wife who had died of grief, and stood to light the candles, one by one; and Hermione had become bright and visible, in the warm, shifting glow. After sixteen years of winter, a barren mountain and perpetual storm, tears shed daily at the grave of a wife and child buried together, Leontes' wife returned to him from death, as music played, as the tree burst into blossom and fruit, a warm and living woman, candles lit to light all the candles that had gone out in their world.

The Wilful Child

Once there was a child who was wilful, and would not do what her mother wished. For this reason, God could find no pleasure in her, and let her become ill. No doctor could do anything to help her, and, in a short time, she died. When she had been lowered into her grave, and the earth covered her over, her arm pushed itself through the earth, refusing to be buried, and stretched upwards. They pushed it below the earth again, and covered it over, but this didn't work: whatever they tried to do, the arm rose up and out of the grave. Then the mother had to go to the grave, and strike at the arm with a stick. When she had done that, the arm was drawn in, and then, at last, the child was at peace, and rested in the earth.

Acknowledgements

I have quoted from the following copyright texts:

The Diary of Anne Frank. (Translated from the Dutch by B. M. Mooyaart-Doubleday. First published 1947 in Holland by Contact, Amsterdam. Copyright 1958 by Vallentine, Mitchell and Co. Ltd.) *Children's Crusade* by Bertolt Brecht. English translation by Hans Keller. Copyright 1969 by Stefan S. Brecht. Reprinted by kind permission of The Estate of Bertolt Brecht. *Emil and the Detectives* by Erich Kästner. (The 1940 edition by Thomas Nelson and Sons Ltd. was published by arrangement with Jonathan Cape Ltd., who first published the novel in 1931.) *The House at Pooh Corner* by A. A. Milne. (Methuen and Co. Ltd.) *The Wind in the Willows* by Kenneth Graham. (Copyright by the University Chest, Oxford.) *A Calendar of German Customs* by Richard Thonger. (Quoted on page 28. Copyright Oswald Wolff (Publishers) Ltd. 1966.) *On the Death of My Child* translated from the German by Leonard Forster. (From *The Penguin Book of German Verse*, page 313. (Copyright Leonard Forster, 1957, 1959. Reprinted by permission of Penguin Books Ltd.) *The Children's Haggadah* was published by Shapiro,

Valentine and Co. in 1937, and was edited by Dr A. M. Silberman.

The versions of the stories by the Brothers Grimm are based upon the translations by Margaret Hunt and James Stern in *The Complete Grimm's Fairy Tales*. (Routledge and Kegan Paul, London 1975. Copyright 1944 by Pantheon Books Inc. Copyright renewed 1972 by Random House, Inc.)

I hope that the dedication at the beginning of this novel, which includes all the above authors, expresses my gratitude to them.

P.S.R.